TWO CHILDREN AND
THEIR JUNGLE ZOO

"Joa can ride with me to town"

TWO CHILDREN
AND
THEIR JUNGLE ZOO

By Rose Brown

Illustrated by Ann Eshner

J. B. LIPPINCOTT COMPANY

PHILADELPHIA · LONDON · NEW YORK

CONTENTS

ILLUSTRATIONS

GUIDE TO PRONUNCIATION OF
PORTUGUESE WORDS

In Portuguese, vowels are generally sounded as follows:—

a *is* ah	*as in* card
e *is hard* a	*as in* crepe
i *is* e	*as in* antique
o *is* o	*as in* lope
u *is* oo	*as in* sue
em *is* aighn	
ti *is* chee	
oia *is* oyah	
y *is* ee	

aldeia	ahl day ah
Altar de Chaõ	Ahl tahr day Shaonh
Alzira	Ahl zay rah
assaí	ah sah ee
atta	ah tah
bacú	bah koo
Beleza	Bay lay zah
bola de macacheira	bo lah day mah kah shay rah
Bom dia	Bone dee ah
Boneca	Bone eh kah
Bonequinho	Bo neh keen yo
Branquissimo	Brahn kee see mo
café	kah fay

campo	kahn po
canaraná	kah nah rah nah
capivara	kah pee vah rah
catorze	kah tor zee
cinco	seehn ko
crèche	kresh
cruzeiro	kroo zay ro
Dá-me esmola	Dah may aysh mo lah
dez	dehsh
Diogo	Dee o go
dois	doish
Dona	Do nah
doze	do zee
Guapo	Gwah po
guarana	gwah rah nah
ilhas de moto	eel yahs day mo to
Itaituba	Ee tah ee too bah
jaboti	zhah bo tee
Joa	Zho ah
José	Zho zeh
machete	mah shay te
Mamai	Mah mah ee
manatee	mah nah tee
marreca	mah rheh kah
Maria	Mah ree ah
mascotte	Mahs caw tee
maté	mah tee
mutum	moo toohn
nene	neh neh
novo	no vo
oito	oy to
onça	ohn sah
onze	ohn zee

Papai	Pah pah ee
Peixe-Boi	Pay she Boy
Pepe	Peh peh
Perla	Pair lah
pirarucú	pee rah roo koo
praça	prah sah
quintal	keehn tahl
quatro	qwah tro
refresco	ray fraysh ko
Respeitavel Publico	Raysh pay tah vehl Poo blee ko
Rio de Janeiro	Ree o day Zhah nay ro
Santarem	Sahn tah raign
sapoti	sah po tee
seis	say eesh
Senhor	Sehn yhor
Sim, êle esta	Seehn ay lee es tah
Serra de Muruaru	Sair rah day Moo roo ah roo
sete	seh tee
Sou uma pobre Cigana	So oohma po bray See gah nah
Tapajoz	Tah pah zhozh
Tatu	Tah too
tatus	tah toosh
tostão	tawsh taonh
três	trayzh
treze	treh zee
tucanaré	too kah nah reh
tucum	too koohn
um	oohn
vamos	vah moosh

TWO CHILDREN AND
THEIR JUNGLE ZOO

I

Jasmina and Jasmine

Creeeak went the wall hooks every time Joa's head popped up out of the blue and white hammock in the quiet shady room. She wriggled and squirmed, for she was trying to see through the doorway. The embroidered white curtain that hung there—to shut out the light but not the air—came just halfway to the floor, for which Joa was very glad. With every slight breeze the curtain swung in and out, giving her quick little views of the wide cool veranda just outside.

Across the cement floor and through the potted plants, Joa

could see bits of the golden beach shimmering in the hot tropical sun of the early afternoon. That is, she could see it when the curtain blew. Evidently something much more important than taking an afternoon nap was going to happen out there. But Joa seemed to be the only one concerned. The other three hammocks, containing the other three members of the Amaral family, just sagged down heavily.

Joa thought that her father and mother and her brother, Tatu, must all be sound asleep. Again her black head popped up from the hammock. Her big, wide-awake, dark brown eyes peered through the white curtain anxiously. *Creeeak* went the wall hooks again.

"Joa, why aren't you asleep yet?" Mamai whispered, peering over the edge of her hammock at Joa. The little girl sat up, which was hard to do without spilling over. She made the motions of climbing out, but her mother shook her head fiercely.

"You lie right down there, Joa. Don't you dare get up yet. And stop looking out. That man won't be here for hours."

"What's the matter with you two?" It was Papai this time who tried to sit up, nearly turned himself out on the floor, and then lay down again out of sight. They heard him grumble a bit, good naturedly, about how he was getting a crick in his neck.

Mamai looked so severely at Joa, putting her finger on her lips at the same time as a warning for quiet, that Joa stretched herself out straight. She could only do this by lying kitty-cornered, which is the way most people sleep in hammocks that have no sticks to keep them open flat. She closed her eyes obediently, thinking Papai and Mamai would be sound asleep

in a minute and then she could peek out again to look for the
man, only more carefully and quietly, not to disturb either of
them. But before she finished even planning this, she was
breathing deeply herself and her eyes did not open again.

Then everything was really quiet, inside and out. Here by
the Amazon River, close to the equator, all men and animals
and even birds drowse through the warm afternoon hours.
Scarcely any sounds could be heard except when one of the
parrots, on the double perch under the veranda eaves, gurgled
and pushed the other for more foot room, or when a hammock hook squeaked as one of the Amaral family attempted
to turn over.

Joa, with her Papai and Mamai and her brother, Tatu, had
arrived only yesterday in Santarem. This little town, several
hundred miles up the Amazon and not far from the Tapajoz
River, had been but a spot on the map of Brazil to any of
them before the government in Rio de Janeiro had asked
Papai to travel through the north and to send the Department
of Agriculture reports of what he thought should be done.
Papai's knowledge of seeds and plants and crops had spread
beyond their own plantation, which was not so very far from
the capital city. There had been a great deal of excitement of
course when the letter came saying that Sr. Amaral could take
the trip accompanied by his wife and two children.

Joa and Tatu had had the thrill of coming all those two
thousand miles by airplanes and by boats, with every mile a
new adventure. Now they were pretty seasoned travelers, but
it was good to settle down in one place for a while. Papai had
a great deal of work to do, but the first day he had found this
nice house for them. He had rented it furnished right away,

along with the parrots, the rest of the pets, the plants and even the servants.

Only the hammocks had to be bought, for the owners of the house had taken theirs with them. Things had moved fast, for Papai was very efficient and Mamai was a good manager, too. Besides, the people of Santarem are the kindest in the world. So within a few hours it seemed to the Amaral family that they had been living there for years. All but the hammocks. And these required a little practice before they could take the place of beds.

It had been fun shopping. In fact, the Amarals always had fun shopping together, for Papai usually let them have what they wanted, and made a lot of jokes. He had led them that day into a store on the main street of Santarem. The store was deep and dusky and cool, and the storekeeper was very accommodating. He had stacks and stacks of hammocks on his shelves. They were all folded neatly with the lace inside. So to really show them the man had to take each one down and open it up. There was no other way to know how big they were. They came in several different sizes, family size, bachelor size, and smaller ones for children. There were even tiny ones for dolls, and people bought these, too, for their pet monkeys. If there is anything a monkey loves, it is to climb into his little hammock and go to sleep swinging, just as if he were back in the treetops. But Papai insisted they should not stop to look at these today, for they all had to find something to sleep in themselves before night. He was not going to miss his after-lunch nap, either.

So the man took down one after another and shook it out with a great flourish. Soon the counters were overflowing. Papai said he was going to have a family size all to himself.

And he was not going to share it with anybody who might turn it upsidedown for him in the middle of the night. He chose a beauty with stripes like a Brazilian rainbow. It had extra wide red, white and blue lace, with fringe and lots of little tassels. After that Mamai said she would take a plain white one which was especially dainty and lacy. Tatu chose a gay one, gay as a macaw, and called it his Joseph's coat of many colors.

"A pretty big coat," Papai had said, wrapping it around him until he was entirely hidden. It was much more like a tent than a coat even for Joseph.

Joa as usual was the last to make up her mind. Finally she picked out a blue and white one, woven in a splashy design, like a Kentucky bed coverlet. On each side was a width of coarse handmade lace, showing a string of boys and girls of white thread worked into the blue background. First a boy and then a girl, then a boy, then a girl, and so on, holding hands just like cutout paper dolls, made from folded paper.

Outside the store door, a man had been waiting who made his living carrying other people's packages. And what a package that was! The storekeeper did not even try to wrap it up, but just folded the four hammocks separately while the Amarals watched. They wanted to learn just how to do it, too, since they might have to pick up their beds and walk at any moment. And then the carrier came in, put the pile on top of his head and marched out. The hammocks were not heavy, but the carrier never could have put his arms around all of them.

Now the whole family was settled and napping sweetly in the hot tropical afternoon.

Their bedroom was very simply furnished. A washstand

with bowl, water pitcher and toilet dishes stood against one wall. Beside it was a small toilet table with curtains and a mirror. And against the other wall was a wardrobe, for houses in such hot countries do not have closets where clothes might grow musty.

There were a couple of straight chairs, besides. But the most important furnishings were the hammock hooks, built into the walls, and the S-shaped holders in each hook that held the rope loops, and made a noise when the hammocks swung.

The front and back walls were almost entirely taken up with double wooden doors.

"Café! Café! Senhor and Madame!" Maria was pushing aside the white curtain, bringing in a little tray with two tiny cups of coffee on it for Papai and Mamai to drink while still in their hammocks. She said Tatu and Joa could each have a glass of milk since there was a dairy right next door. It was very clean and neat she added, so the milk was safe and fresh, which is not always true in hot places. Both children were wide awake then. They hung their legs over the edges of their beds and began to swing. Higher and higher—until Tatu bumped right into Mamai, and nearly upset her coffee. But Mamai only laughed and told them to sit still or they would spill the milk all over themselves. Maria was just coming in with their glasses. This was the first thing she had ever done for Tatu and Joa. She smiled and waited for them to finish. Her fresh white clothes smelled sweet with Santarem sachet. She asked how old they were. And she said she had a young brother and sister about their ages, except that the sister was the age of Tatu and the brother the age of Joa. Her family lived near by, so they would all meet soon.

Then she went out with the glasses and tray, and came right back again.

"There is a man waiting to see you, Senhor," she told Papai. "He says there is no hurry."

Before Papai could say, "I'll be right out," Joa gave one glance through the door and shrieked with excitement, leaped down and ran out on the veranda. How could she have forgotten about this important man?

There he stood at the veranda steps holding the bridle of the most adorable horse Joa had ever seen. It was small and brown, and its ears were tiny and pointed. It wore a star on its forehead, and one white stocking. It kept nuzzling the man with its nervous velvety nose.

Joa just stood still and looked. This lovely creature was going to be hers, the first horse she had ever owned all by herself!

Papai came out, looking pleased. He began to talk about buying the horse, how much it was, and whether it was really safe for a little girl who had not learned to ride very well yet. Joa thought she could ride quite well for her size. Of course not like Tatu, who was three years older. But she did not interrupt to say so. Then the man leaped into the saddle without even touching the stirrup. And away went the little animal like a streak down the beach and back again. It was single-footing so nicely and stopped so gently that the man scarcely moved at all.

"You see," he said to Papai, "her gait is as easy as swinging in a hammock."

"That's true," Papai agreed, putting out his hand to feel

how silky the brown coat was. He ran his fingers down the smooth legs that had learned to move so cleverly. "All right," he said at last, reaching into his pocket for his billfold. "I'll buy her. If she's too lively for my little girl, then my boy can ride her and maybe you can find her something else."

Then Joa spoke up. "Please let me try, Papai." She could not bear for anyone else to have her horse.

Papai turned around. Joa had been so quiet he had forgotten she was there.

"That's a good idea. We might settle it right away," he said. "This sandy beach is so soft you won't get hurt if you do fall off."

But Joa would not fall. She could not let herself fall. She was quite determined about that. This was going to be a test, and she would show them!

Papai lifted Joa into the saddle and put the reins into her hands. Then he adjusted the stirrups for her short legs.

"There you are," he said, when all was ready.

"What's her name?" asked Joa.

"Jasmina," answered the man. "That is because she is so sweet, and because she has a star jasmine on her forehead."

"Vamos, Jasmina!" said Joa quietly. And again the little horse was off like a shot, almost taking Joa's breath away. But the saddle under her was steady as a table. There really was not the slightest danger. She turned her mount around nicely, and came back with hair blowing and colors flying, feeling as if she had won a race.

Mamai and Tatu and Maria had all come out onto the veranda to watch by this time. And Papai was looking proud, as she let him help her slide to the sands.

"Jasmina is yours. And say! You're quite a horsewoman already," he said, tying the bridle to one of the veranda posts. "And now what can you find for my son?" he asked the man. "Tatu would like something a little bigger, I guess—more his size. Eh, Tatu?" For Tatu was looking envious and rather left out of things.

Yes, the man knew of just the animal, in fact, one that his own son had been riding. It was arranged that he would return next day from his farm several miles down the beach. So he said good-by to them all, with a special good-by to Jasmina, who nuzzled her nose against him so affectionately that he kissed the white star between her eyes.

"Be a good girl, Jasmina, and a good friend to Joa," he said. "I think you'll get on fine together."

Joa wanted to start right off on Jasmina, but Papai said no, Jasmina had to be shod first. Besides, Joa would not be allowed to ride alone at first. Joa was disappointed for a moment. But far down the beach toward the town people were coming across the sands for their afternoon dip. And Maria came to ask the Amarals if they had seen how clear and beautiful the river was today? That was because the water from the Tapajoz was in.

Although this was five hundred miles from the Atlantic Ocean, the tide rose and fell twice a day, with the hour always changing just like tides along a sea beach. Just now it was out, so the Tapajoz River came rushing down into the Amazon, all green and clear. That made it nice for bathing.

"After the tide turns," Maria said, "the muddy yellow water

of the main river will push the green water back in its place. Now it is just perfect. But it will grow muddy again soon, so you had better hurry."

They all rushed indoors while Mamai tried to remember in just which piece of baggage she had packed the bathing suits. She tumbled through several suitcases before she found them. And then she looked around at the disorder, with clothes on the hammocks and some on the floor.

"I'd better stay here and unpack," she said.

"No, you don't," said Papai, shoving everything back into the bags regardless of wrinkles. "We'll all help you after dinner."

The beach in front of their house was a highway for people afoot and on horseback. It led to the farms that faced the river for several miles beyond. There was always someone passing. And there were also canoes going up to the town for shopping and coming back full of purchases. They kept near shore to avoid the current. So it was really like a double highway, half water and half land, quite lively and interesting.

But for bathing they had a private beach. The water was cool and refreshing, and they had a lot of fun splashing each other, and taking short swims. People in canoes passed them, always saying, "Good afternoon," very politely. Then they lay on the sands in slanting sunlight that was not hot any more.

"What does our house look like from here?" asked Papai.

"It doesn't look much like our real home down south," said Mamai.

"It's like an excursion boat," said Tatu, "except it has a red tile roof and no smokestack."

"That's what I was thinking," said Papai. "The great veranda running around it is like the deck. And our bedroom —I mean hammock-room—and sitting room, the kitchen and the rest, are like the lounge and cabins on a steamboat. And our dining room being out on the deck makes it just like a pleasure boat."

"Maybe we'll float away in the night," said Joa. "That would be fun."

"You think it would?" Mamai shivered. "The trouble is, it might come true. I've read of too many houses being swept away when these rivers let loose. And it's no fun, Joa."

"And here in Santarem the Amazon rises thirty feet," Papai added.

Finally Mamai said, "May I be excused now?" And Papai got up and pulled her to her feet.

"I'll go with you to help unpack and you won't need the children," he said.

In a few minutes Mamai came to the door, all dressed, and called across the veranda.

"Come here, children, I want to show you something." She looked as if she had a surprise for them and they came running.

"Go open the door of the wardrobe," Mamai said mysteriously.

"Is there something in there that will jump out at me? A snake maybe?" asked Joa hanging back.

But Tatu was already opening the door a little and peeking in.

"Oh, oh! How nice!" he said, his nose deeper in the crack. Joa crowded behind him trying to see, while he teased her by making pleased noises. "What lovely snakes! Um-m-m-m! St-st-s-s" he hissed, until Joa's curiosity completely got the better of her and she reached under his arm and pulled the door wide open.

The whole room was suddenly filled with the most delightful odor.

"M-m-m-m," sniffed Joa. "It is as sweet as—Jasmina!" For Maria had scattered fresh star jasmine flowers all over the floor of the wardrobe and laid packets of sachet there to mix with the nice spicy odor of the cedar wood of the wardrobe. Mamai said this was surely a beautiful Santarem custom, as they all helped put their things on hangers and then shut them up with the perfume.

II

Bonequinho Disappears

NEXT MORNING the Amaral family was up at the first light. The sun rises at exactly six o'clock all the year around at the equator, and sets at six, too; so the nights and days are always equal. Today especially the Amarals wanted to enjoy the coolest hours.

Papai said he was going to take a rough ride in a truck to the government experimental farm where he had business. And he would take Jasmina to the blacksmith and get her two pairs of iron shoes so she could run on the stone streets. Mamai said she was going to get acquainted with her house and find out where the good dinner came from that Maria had put on the table the night before. And Tatu and Joa had so many fascinating things to do and see that they couldn't say just where they would start.

Papai suggested they could begin by learning to make their beds. He set the example by unhooking one end of his own, rolling it, tying its ropes around it, and leaving the roll dangling from the other hook. Then he taught the children how to do it. The hammocks looked funny hanging in four bundles in a row along one wall. And Papai said that this

Indian invention for folding beds was better than anything the white men had thought up.

When the children saw the green water was in, they could hardly wait to eat their rolls and drink their coffee, which was mostly hot milk. They were going to play in the river and on the beach all morning.

"Look out for sting rays," said Mamai. "For they can hide in the muddy yellow water." But just now the water was perfect.

"Was anybody ever stung by a sting ray?" asked Tatu. He had heard of this horrible skate, a flat fish with a devil's face, that carried a toothed barb in the side of its tail. There was a picture of it in his zoology book at home.

"Yes, I know a man who was stung once. He stepped on a sting ray by accident in the yellow water. He had to walk on crutches for a month and he still limps, I think. But they won't chase you. They just lie in wait to catch fish for their dinners, and use their sting tail to defend themselves," replied Mamai.

"I'd love to see one," said Tatu.

"Now, promise me you won't go looking for them," said Mamai, "or I'll be nervous every minute we are here."

"The fishermen catch them in their nets sometimes, Tatu," said Mamai. "I'll ask our fish man to bring you a dead one. And now if you children want to go bathing, I'll bring the towels."

Tatu promised Mamai he would keep away from sting rays. He and Joa had the beach all to themselves, just like yesterday. They splashed and paddled and sailed leaf boats.

They ran swimming races which Tatu always won unless he pretended to lose.

Then something began happening to the river. The yellow water was moving up. It was making a strong wavy line where it hit the green. There were swirls and little whirlpools where sticks and leaves jigged around. In a few minutes the two waters were fighting, the yellow driving the green back a few feet at a time. It was like a battle line, sure enough, Tatu thought. And then the yellow water came rushing toward them. And the green water was running away, up the stream, back to its bed in the Tapajoz. It was very interesting to watch. And suddenly they were standing in the yellow water.

"Ouch!" yelled Joa. "I felt a sting ray!"

Her "sting ray" came to the surface then, and it was a green twig with sharp thorns growing on it, like a piece of the needle tree. It had barely grazed her leg, just enough to let her know it was sharp, without scratching her. But that reminded Tatu of his promise to Mamai.

"We have to go out now, I guess," he said, regretfully.

"But we can play on the beach, can't we?" asked Joa.

So they buried each other in the sand, and built castles, and hunted for river shells and pretty stones. Tatu was always looking for pumice which is rare and precious, for it comes from the faraway Andes where the volcanoes spit it out. Tatu told Joa how it must take years for a piece of this light lava stone to bump a short distance at a time down the Andes, when there are big rains, until it finally reaches some little stream. But it goes fast enough when it hits the big river, for sometimes the current travels twelve miles an hour and even a lot faster in the rainy season. So it floats down at the rate of a couple of hundred miles a day. Tatu thought this ought to be a good place to find some, because the waters were always moving around here.

Joa did not care much for Tatu's rocks. The only thing she collected was dolls. So she soon grew tired and lay down in the sun to rest. But Tatu kept on. And finally he did find a small piece of the gray porous stone. When he washed the sand off, he could see that something had once been carved on it—the face of an animal. But the water had worn the features almost flat. Just the same, it was a fine specimen, and a real treasure to add to his collection of everything interesting from this part of the country. He was satisfied now and lay down to rest beside his sister and thoroughly to examine his precious pumice stone.

Suddenly there was a soft sound in the sand behind Joa, and a warm wind fanned her face. She opened her eyes. A monstrous black head with red nostrils and horns was hanging over her. It was breathing on her, smelling her hair. A huge beast big as a house was almost on top of her. She screamed and grabbed her brother. Tatu gave one look, leaped to his feet and dragged Joa after him. It was hard running through the deep sand and pulling Joa along. She seemed to stick in every one of her foot-steps. But he kept on without glancing back until they were safe on the veranda. Nothing was following them. But Maria came running, for she had heard Joa's scream.

They both stopped, panting, beside her, still badly scared. Back there on the beach where they had been lying stood

It was hard running through the deep sand and pulling Joa along

a huge, inky-black bull with great hunched shoulders like a buffalo. Tatu was pointing at it, showing it to Maria, and the bull was staring back at him.

"Why, that's only Peixe-Boi," said Maria, "up to his tricks again. You don't need to be afraid of him. We call him sea cow or manatee because he's so fat and harmless."

"I thought he was going to eat me," said Joa.

"He wouldn't hurt a soul. In fact, he has become such a great pet that we have all spoiled him."

"He's an awfully big pet," Tatu laughed.

"He is a very smart pet," Maria explained. "And we mustn't let him think you are afraid of him or he will figure out a good way to have fun out of that. Look at the rascal!" she said. "He is standing there wondering why you children acted so queer."

"Anybody would act queer," said Tatu, "if they looked up into snorting red nostrils and big horns."

"Of course they would if they did not know Peixe-Boi. You children come along with me right now and get acquainted," said Maria, taking each of them by the hand.

Tatu was beginning to feel a bit sheepish, so he went forward, although he did not really want to. But Joa was still scared and only marched along because Maria had tight hold of her hand.

Peixe-Boi took a step or two toward them. He looked bigger than ever, with his great buffalo hump and square black body. But he went on chewing his cud, very contented.

"Nice old Peixe-Boi!" murmured Maria. She dropped Tatu's hand and began to scratch the creature's back. Then she rubbed the spot between his horns. He loved it.

"See, he is like Fernando the Bull," said Maria. "He is gentle as a kitten. He would purr if he knew how."

"Could I pet him?" asked Tatu, quickly getting over his fear.

"Of course. Try it."

So Tatu did like Maria, scratched the broad flat back and the curly place between the bull's horns. Even Joa came near enough to reach out a hand and smooth his thick neck. The skin was so loose and the hair so soft, it was almost like a cloak. For Peixe-Boi was a very fine animal of a special Oriental breed which likes tropical countries, and he was worth a lot of money, even if they did call him sea cow.

Suddenly Peixe-Boi lifted his head and sniffed the air like Fernando smelling the flowers. Two canoes were crossing from the other side of the river. The canoers were paddling hard to keep from being swept downstream by the swirling yellow water. And a boy and an old man were doing something strange with logs at the water's edge near by. They were using poles as levers, rolling the logs into the river. Then they walked in after them, and floated them around and knotted short ropes around them until they made a hollow square. The beach made one side of the square. The canoes came steadily in toward the shore. And when they were nearer, Tatu and Joa saw they were filled with coarse green grass that is called "false sugar cane."

They pulled up to the logs and threw the grass into the hollow square. It floated and looked so inviting that Peixe-Boi left the children and lumbered toward his dinner. This was what he had been waiting for all the time while he was amusing himself with Tatu and Joa.

He walked right into the water and began to eat the grass off the top of it. And at that moment someone let out a lot of cows. They came trotting across the beach, all of them hungry. Tatu counted. There were fifteen. All walked into the cool water and began nibbling at the floating grass with Peixe-Boi. They were getting a bath and a dinner at the same time.

One last cow was taking her time. She was the only spotted one in the herd—white with big black splashes on her. Her horns were long and one of them was crooked. When she spied Maria and the children she stopped to look at them. Then she came walking toward them.

"Oh," Joa gasped. "She is coming after us."

"Don't be such a fraidy cat," said Tatu. He was brave enough himself now he had grown used to Peixe-Boi. "You can see she is tame as anything. Isn't she, Maria?"

"She is the tamest one of all," answered Maria. "That is the reason her name is Boneca (Bone-eh-kah—which means doll in Portuguese). She doesn't look much like a doll now, but when she was a calf she was the prettiest little thing."

Boneca came a little farther and stopped, as Maria and the children went to meet her. All she wanted was a little petting, like Peixe-Boi. But she did hope they had something in their pockets for her, besides.

At that moment a terrific racket started behind the house somewhere. Such a bawling and caterwauling!

"Those are the dairy calves," explained Maria. "They want to get out, too. But they can't, for they would keep their mothers from eating." Several mammas lifted their heads, and looked anxiously toward their babies. One of them bawled back. And that started the calves all over again.

By this time the canoes were paddling home across the river to where the men lived who cut the green hay and sold it to the dairy.

The old man and the boy came walking up the beach now. Their cotton pants were still rolled up and splashed with water. Maria introduced them. This was Senhor Diogo and his grandson, José. They took care of the cows at the dairy, and maybe they would show Tatu and Joa the calves who had been making such a fuss.

"Our babies," José called them.

"Our cry-babies," corrected Sr. Diogo laughing. "Just listen to them. You would think their hearts were breaking."

"Come on. Let's go comfort them," said José, starting down a runway between two fences.

The calves were sticking their muzzles through the pen behind the house next door. And when they saw friends coming they stopped bawling and wanted to be petted.

"Um—dois—três—one, two, three, four——fifteen!" Tatu counted, just as he had counted the cows. "Why, there is a calf for each cow."

"Yes," said Sr. Diogo, "we let each cow keep her baby. We never take them away until they are so old the mother doesn't mind."

They surely were pretty. Some of them were fawn colored, some gray. And one was spotted black and white. This was Bonequinho, son of Boneca. Their noses were very wet, their hides were silky and loose, and their skin hung in soft folds around their necks, for these calves all had Oriental blood.

The children put their hands through the bars and patted

first one, then the other. Such rough tongues as they stuck out trying to lick Tatu's and Joa's hands and faces!

But now they were more interested in their mothers, who had finished eating and were coming back into their corral, one at a time. This meant that the calves could be let out, and they knew it. So the minute the last cow was inside and the bars were up, José opened the calf-pen gate, and the little fellows went scampering down the runway like a lot of puppies. Their tails flew out behind them and when they reached the beach they ran races. Several of them stopped to leap into the water, or to take a nibble of grass and a drink. And then they raced after the others away down the beach.

Now came the turn of the cows to bawl. They gathered at the bars and called after their children. "Don't go away!" "Don't go far!" "Come back!" "Come back!" they cried. The one that bawled loudest was Boneca.

But the calves never answered a word. They only ran farther and faster, like naughty babies. And the one that ran the fastest was little spotted Bonequinho.

"Go after them, José! Don't let any of them get lost," said Sr. Diogo.

"May I go, too?" asked Tatu.

But Tatu did not wait for permission. He raced after José who was running after the calves. It became a game now. At least the calves thought it was, for they chased down the beach having a lot of fun beating their two-legged opponents. They ran and they ran and they ran, until they were too tired to go any farther. Only then did José and Tatu catch up with them. By this time, too, the boys were panting and the sun was hot. Their legs felt weak from racing through the deep sand. So they rounded the animals up in a little herd and sat down. Some of the calves sat down, too. And everything was quite calm as the boys began to count. "Um, dois, três, quatro, cinco, seis, sete, oito, nove, dez, onze, doze, treze, catorze—"

But where was number fifteen? They counted again—fourteen! One was missing. How could it have got away? So they counted once more. It was gone, all right.

Far away, back at the house, they could hear the mothers bawling. The calves lifted up their heads to listen. Maybe the missing one would hear, too, and want to go home. Which one was gone? José checked them over, so many gray ones —so many white ones—so many tan ones—but no black and white. It was Bonequinho who was gone.

José began to worry. Sr. Diogo had always told him this would happen some day if he did not watch out, that they would run too far and not be able to get back. And now it had happened. The calves were his especial care and he had lost one.

Tatu began to look under the bushes. No Bonequinho.

"That doesn't do any good," said José. "If he were here he would come out. He would want to know what we are doing. He is the most curious thing." José sounded so discouraged.

And then they saw Sr. Diogo coming. He was hurrying, and looking worried.

He said José must hunt for Bonequinho until he found him. And he must be quick about it, for if the calf got away from the river's edge farther down, there was a jungle. Then an alligator or an onça (spotted leopard) would get him. That jungle was full of them.

"Run, José! Hurry!" said Sr. Diogo.

"I'm going to help him," offered Tatu.

"All right. I'll drive the rest of the calves back home before they get into more trouble. They are full of mischief today. I don't know what has got into them."

III

In the Jungle

TATU AND JOSÉ did not stop to watch Sr. Diogo drive the calves back or they would have been surprised. He could not get them started. They were too tired and did not want to go. Some lay down. Others tried to go the wrong way. He had to push them along, talk to them, beg them.

Meanwhile José and Tatu were peering into every bit of beach brush where Bonequinho could hide. José kept calling, "Bonequinho! Bonequinho!"

They came to a little farm where there was a palm leaf hut. A woman was sitting out in front mending her husband's shirt.

"Good morning, Dona Anna. Have you seen our black and white calf, Bonequinho?" asked José.

Dona Anna was very polite. She was sorry the calf was lost, she said. But she had been inside her house all morning until just now, so Bonequinho might have gone by without her knowing it.

They passed a man loping along on a gray horse. He was carrying a letter in his hand ready for the mail box.

"Bom dia, Senhor Roberto," said José. "Our black and

white calf is lost. Have you seen him?"

"No, I haven't," answered Sr. Roberto. "But when I come back from the post office I'll help you look for him."

Then came some fishermen, carrying their nets and a string of fish they had caught by casting from the beach. They had not seen Bonequinho, either. But they had been busy with their fishing and might not have noticed.

Tatu wanted to stop and look at their fish, but José hurried him along.

A canoe came past loaded with a family—mother and father with three small children. They were strangers from far away, said José.

"Bon dia, Senhor e Senhora," he called to them. "Have you seen a black and white spotted calf along the shore? We have lost him."

No, they hadn't. But they had just crossed the river from the other side.

So no one had seen Bonequinho. And now Tatu and José were coming to the little jungle Sr. Diogo had warned them about. It had been easy hunting Bonequinho along the sandy beach, but how could they ever find him in this wild place, even if the alligators and the jaguars had not got him already?

After the bright sun on the water, they could see nothing in the dusky shade at first. Then they could make out the path where Sr. Roberto had just come along with his letter. It ran parallel to the river only a few yards away. His horse's hoof prints were filling up with water. But there were no calf tracks. Besides, Bonequinho could not be along this path or the man would have seen him. José said he had been here before, lots of times. After awhile you came out on a beach again if you went far enough.

José said they would have to go back to the beach and try another path. The second path was dry and sandy at first. It went away from the beach up a little rise. And here were plenty of tracks of cloven hooves.

"Look!" Tatu cried out. "He's been here!"

But José was not so sure. He said the tracks looked more like wild pigs' hoof marks. Still—he was not sure. Both boys examined them carefully, for Tatu knew what wild pigs' foot prints looked like. There were lots of those animals at home down south, on his father's plantation.

"You must have awfully big wild pigs here, with feet like Bonequinho's!" he said.

But José said he thought they just looked big because of the loose sand. Anyway, they would follow the tracks for a little way and see.

The trail grew fainter and fainter as it went downhill and then over fallen leaves. Twice there were little branches going off to the side.

"We had better mark this place or we'll be getting lost," said Tatu.

"Oh, we can find our way back all right," José answered. "I've been in this jungle lots of times."

Nevertheless, Tatu tied his handkerchief to a branch where two trails crossed. Here they did not know just which one to take, for both were so small and faint. Besides the swinging vines and branches overhead now hung so low the boys had to bend over to get through.

"Pretty soon Bonequinho can't get through here, either," said Tatu, bending lower and lower. And then came the tracks again, but clearly now. For the ground was growing more moist as it ran downhill. Below them there was a glint of sunshine on a shiny pond where the trail widened out to water. Both boys dropped to their knees. And sure enough, Tatu now saw that these were pig tracks, much smaller than any calf would make.

The boys looked at each other, completely discouraged now.

"Sh-sh—listen—" Something was coming—the sound of thudding feet on the soft path. There was just time to jump back behind the trunk of a great tree. Along came the softly thudding noises. Then there was a gentle grunting such as wild pigs make when they jostle each other. And two of these creatures came into sight, trotting steadily along. Then surely the boys knew that this was only a pig track leading down to their drinking place.

The pigs stopped in front of the spot where the boys were hiding—suspicious, grunting to each other. But fortunately a slight breeze was blowing from the other direction. The boys were down wind and the pigs could not smell them.

Neither Tatu nor José would have been afraid of two wild pigs, if there were only two. But the next thing that happened was just what they had imagined. The two pigs went down to the water and foraged around a bit. Then they gave their signal. Down this path, and out of several others came a whole stampede of wild pigs. The word had been grunted by the two scouts that the coast was clear. And the pack was thirsty. The pigs squealed and grunted, fought and pushed each other off the paths. They came tumbling out of the bushes from every direction with their mouths open, their sharp white tusks showing. In a minute the whole pond seemed to be full of pigs. The water was nothing but mud. There must have been fifty of them. And they had no idea that a human being was anywhere near them.

The boys watched, fascinated. Although they had lived all their lives where wild hogs were plentiful, neither of them had ever seen more than two or three at a time. They had heard how these pigs live in packs, and how dangerous such a pack is if it becomes excited. Why, even a jaguar is afraid of a lot of these hogs together. While he is killing a couple of them, the rest can tear him to pieces. And a young calf like Bonequinho would have had no chance at all if they were very hungry.

"We had better get out of here before they get wind of us," whispered José.

Tatu nodded, and motioned for José to go ahead. He was trying to remember just where he had tied that white handkerchief.

Quiet as a mouse, not stirring a leaf with his bare toes, José slipped out onto the path. But Tatu was not so fortunate, for he was wearing shoes. He rattled some twigs, stood still a moment to pick out better spots for his feet, and instantly the hogs were silent, too. They had heard him. Then he listened to the sound of their scouts' footsteps. They were coming to investigate. Tatu leaped out of his tracks and sped back over the path with the rat-tat-tat of the pigs behind him. José was already out of sight, but Tatu caught up with him in a minute and left the pigs behind. So the sentinels, thinking they had chased an enemy safely away, told the rest of the pigs they could go back to their wallowing and drinking. Tatu could hear them again, squealing at each other.

There was just time to jump back behind the trunk of a great tree

José was standing at a crisscross of trails, examining them closely. Now he knew that all these paths were only animals' roads used by the wild folk of the jungle to travel from their lairs to a drinking or feeding place. Perhaps none of them led to the beach. Tatu bent over the spot, too. Neither of them could remember being here before. And there was no way to tell what direction to take. They looked up through the high trees, all covered with vines and orchids. A tiny glint of light showed that the sun was directly overhead. It was noon, for here on the equator the sun travels in an arc exactly across the middle of the sky, and never goes to the north or the south with the seasons as it does in our country.

They were afraid to yell because of attracting the hogs.

"Well, here we are," José said, smiling at his little joke.

Since it did not seem to make any difference which direction they took, they decided to explore all the little runways, separately. Tatu took one, José another. In a minute both were back at the starting place. José said his had ended in the bushes. But Tatu reported that there was a clearing a little farther along, where a great tree had fallen. At least they could watch the sun here and the direction it was traveling toward the west. Once they got their bearings they would know which way to turn toward home.

The clearing was very pretty. It would be a lovely place to play, hidden in the middle of the forest. Great vines hung down in loops like ropes. Here were perfect swings all ready to be swung in. The thick leafy branches of the fallen tree made caves to play robber in. The long trunk still attached to the broken stump was wonderful for a balancing act. There were natural trapezes and spring boards. Here was everything for a circus, with the menagerie ready to start squealing and roaring back in the woods. The tent was the surrounding trees, all ready and waiting for the actors. And Tatu and José were the actors—except they were too worried just now to perform.

They sat down on the fallen tree to rest and talk things over. Both of them were tired. And they had so many problems of their own that they had forgotten all about poor little Bonequinho, who even now couldn't be much more lost than they themselves were.

Never was anything so slow as that sun, which seemed not to move at all. The boys waited, knowing that as soon as it cast a shadow they must find a path going in the opposite direction. At first they talked mostly about how Indians never got lost in the forest like this. How they always noticed all the little things, such as how a twig grew crooked, or how a stone was turned on edge, or where there was moss or a stain on a tree. Every few feet an Indian's kodak mind took a picture. Afterward he could retrace his steps exactly by these tiny things he remembered. And now José and Tatu were willing to admit they had remembered practically nothing. So they stopped talking and just watched the ground for the sun to cast a shadow.

Things were so quiet in their forest room, or circus tent, that the birds began to move about and chirp, just as if they were alone. One flew overhead and dropped a bit of palm fruit right in Tatu's lap. There were several berries attached to a branch.

"I'm hungry," said Tatu, suddenly remembering the lunch he was missing.

"I am, too," chimed in José.

"Here. Help yourself." Tatu held out the fruit and José broke off several berries.

There was not much to eat on them, each being mostly one big seed with a little pulp growing around it. But the taste was nice and nutty, good enough to make them hungrier. José got up and began to look around for something more. They both peered into the thick bushes for fruit or nuts, and pretty soon José spied a small tree with globes of green fruit hanging in it, about the size of oranges. This kind of fruit grows wild only around Santarem. And at first Tatu would not believe it was a fruit. It looked more like a very warty pine cone starting to open. José said it was called *atta*. And it was tasty. They were lucky to find a young tree with low limbs. He broke off one of the rough balls and Tatu would scarcely believe anything so hard and green could be ripe. But when José smashed the crust it was just like perfumed custard inside. In fact this was the wild brother of the custard apples that grew in the orchards at Tatu's home. And it certainly was good.

So Tatu went to pick several for himself. But when he reached up into the tree, he was greeted with squawks of protest. For two parakeets decided they were not going to have more of their attas stolen by these two boys. They made a big fuss until Tatu began to coax them to make friends. Then they sidled along the limb quite near him. They were talking in gurgles now, wanting to make friends, too. Tatu put out his hand and they stepped onto his finger, one after the other. They paddled up his arm and sat together on his shoulder, as if they belonged there and intended to stay.

Of course these could not be wild parakeets, the boys agreed. They were somebody's pets which had strayed to the woods and wanted to find a master again. Tatu and José fed the birds with atta while they ate some themselves. And José insisted they belonged to Tatu; since they had picked him out of their own accord. Tatu said he would like to own them. But perhaps they would want to stay in the forest, after all, when the time came to go.

And this reminded them that they were only waiting for the sun to show them how to go home. The birds had been so amusing that they had forgotten to watch. Now they noticed that their own shadows lay short on the ground, pointing from west to east.

They had really grown to like this lovely place. They decided if they ever got safely home they would come again and play here. They could always climb the fallen tree if the wild pigs discovered them. Meanwhile, they would keep it secret and only for themselves. And they would always be friends and have a lot of fun.

This time they really did mark the path, like Indians, remembering where there was a big ant hill, where a queer sort of palm stood, and just how the runways crisscrossed. It all seemed very simple. But their chosen path to the west suddenly turned and took them deeper and deeper into the forest. According to the sun, they were going due south, away from the river. And now both José and Tatu began to be frightened. What if they never did get out?

Back they went once more to the crossroads, the birds sitting contentedly on Tatu's shoulder, actually going to sleep.

Then they heard shouting. A man's voice off in the distance

yelled, "Halloo! Halloo! José! Oh, José!"

"It's my grandfather!" exclaimed José joyfully. "Grandpa! Grandpa! Who—ooo-ooo!" he called back. And then he kept on yelling, so Sr. Diogo could follow the sound and locate them.

They heard him coming, shouting nearer and nearer. They ran down the trail toward his voice, that was coming from just the opposite direction they had been trying to go. And when he appeared, he was carrying his machete, and in his belt was his revolver. He was too glad to see them to start scolding. Indeed, he began to blame himself for not forbidding the boys to go to the forest.

"I started out worrying about Bonequinho, and ended up by being terribly worried about you two," he explained. "Then Senhora Amaral called Tatu for lunch. And when he could not be found and I had to explain I had let him go off on a calf hunt with my grandson, I was in trouble for sure. For she began to be nervous and we all got scared. Why didn't you answer when I first called? I nearly yelled myself hoarse."

"We did as soon as we heard you."

"We never did find Bonequinho," said Tatu. "The poor thing! Maybe the wild pigs got him."

"Maybe—" said Sr. Diogo. "But I doubt it. He probably never got this far, judging from the way the others were played out."

It was the hottest part of the afternoon. The way back seemed twice as long as it had before, for instead of stopping to rest, they kept taking little side trips, still hoping to find the lost calf. Only the little parrots took things easy, dozing away on Tatu's shoulder.

When at last they came in sight of the house, Mamai was waiting anxiously on the veranda. She was very cross because Tatu had gone away without telling her. She would scarcely look at the parakeets. Joa was already taking her siesta. Mamai said Tatu was not to wake her even to show her the new pets. If Tatu wanted something to eat, the cook had kept something hot for him. And there was plenty for José and Sr. Diogo, too, she added, because Brazilians are always hospitable. Then she smiled at Tatu at last. He said he was sorry, and kissed her hand, as Brazilians do. And she said she was sorry she was cross.

They all walked around toward the kitchen after that. And who should be standing there but Bonequinho, saucy as anything, switching his tail at the bars next door!

"However did he get here?" exclaimed José, pleased and angry at the same time. He could see Boneca reaching her head through the bars to lick the young rascal every time he came near enough. There he was, giving frisky leaps, all full of play again and ready to lead the boys another merry chase.

"Just another calf trick, I guess," replied Sr. Diogo to the question on both their faces. "He was probably here all the time, hiding behind the corral. And when he got good and ready, he ambled out to see his mother."

IV

Tatu Meets the Animals

THE COOK had saved some nice nourishing soup which she put on the kitchen table, three big soup plates full. Tatu, José and Sr. Diogo sat down. Then she took three little steaks out of her screened food box. She laid them on her meat board and gave them a good pounding with her meat mallet. First she beat them with the spiked side that looked like a giant's war club, then with the smooth side to flatten them out again. By that time they were quite thin. And they were very tender. She picked up her fan made out of braided palm leaf strips and fanned her fire until the flame died down. When there was nothing but hot glowing coals, she laid the steaks on the coals, and in a minute she flipped them over to cook the other side. While this was happening, she cracked three eggs and slid them into a pan where they sizzled in hot fat. By the time the plates of soup were empty, all was ready. Each steak lay in the middle of its plate in a nest of shredded lettuce, with a shaky white and gold egg on top.

The cook knew, too, that eggs and beef make boys very strong. So while she stood off and watched them eat, she smiled. She was fat and jolly, and quite nice to look at, her big apron spotless in spite of all the fanning of ashes on the open hearth of her stove. For this was no stove made of iron, covered with white enamel like those they have in cities. It was built of stones cemented together, with separate holes for little fires, such as she had just used for broiling the steaks. In her jet black hair was a sprig of star jasmine. And her black eyes were big and shining. Sr. Diogo called her Dona Alzira.

She did not have much time to watch them eat, though, for the steak and eggs were gone in no time. And she had to serve the next course, boiled yellow squash, which came out of a big red cooking jar. It tasted of the tiny specks of green herb Tatu could see scattered through it. Right on top of his serving was a whole clove.

Cook was not looking on this time. She was busy making the dessert, which was a very simple one. She split two ripe avocado pears, emptied out the green pulp, mashed it with sugar, squeezed a lime over it, then she beat it until it was light and resembled pistachio ice cream. But Tatu knew quite well that this mixture would not be a bit cold. And he could taste it in advance, for it was a favorite dessert back home on the plantation.

The two parakeets, still on Tatu's shoulder, could smell the rich avocado odor and they started to climb down. So he held up a teaspoonful, first to one little parrot then the other. Dona Alzira laughed and brought him a fresh spoon. And when they wiped their bills on his coat, she cleaned the places with the corner of her apron. So it was not spotless any more.

While they finished their dessert, the boys talked about nice names for the parakeets, a boy's name and a girl's name suited to their size. José thought of Pepe for the boy, because

Pepe was the nickname of someone who was always up to cute little tricks like those they were going to teach the boy parakeet. And then, of course, Nene would have to be the name of the girl, because that went with Pepe. Thus the parakeets got their names of Pepe and Nene.

After that was settled, the boys asked to be excused. While Sr. Diogo drank his coffee, they went out on the kitchen porch. This was the first time Tatu had been at the back of the house, and what he saw was fascinating.

There was an orchard with all sorts of fruit trees. Tatu recognized a lot of these. There were oranges and limes and sweet lemons. There was a big sapoti tree, and another full of the avocados that had furnished their dessert. And still another was heavy with custard apples. Pomegranate bushes and coffee shrubs were both red with fruit. Besides these, there were a number Tatu had never seen before. In fact, there were too many trees to look carefully at all of them now.

In the middle of the orchard Tatu could see a vegetable garden standing on legs like a great table. It was full of growing things, for that is the way vegetables are grown in Santarem. The gardener must build a platform high above the ground and fill it with rich earth about a foot thick. This is necessary because plants have too many insect enemies living in and on the ground that devour young seedlings before they can start to grow.

This vegetable platform had radishes, lettuce, collards, spinach, Swiss chard, tomatoes, and a lot of the green herbs that are used for flavoring.

But Tatu scarcely glanced at these things, for a whole flock of wild birds ran off when they saw a stranger, and stood looking at him from a safe distance. There was a gray monkey, too, sitting on the rail of the porch making faces at him. And under the trees were various pens and shelters of palm leaves where pets were peeking out to see what had frightened the birds. Papai had said they were renting the pets along with the house. Papai had laughed when he said that. And now Tatu knew why.

"This is almost like a zoo!" exclaimed Tatu, very much excited.

"I never saw a zoo," said José, "but we've lots of animals here. Come and I'll show them to you so they won't be afraid of you." José felt quite at home in Tatu's house, being such a near neighbor.

José took a handful of corn out of a basket on the porch, gave it to Tatu, and put several handfuls in his own pockets. He threw a few grains on the ground, and the birds came running. The biggest one was a mutum turkey. This is a Brazilian wild turkey, a glistening black bird with big red wattles on top of his head. Of course the mutum was greedy and wanted all the corn for himself. The other birds were afraid of him, too. So José picked him up and held him so he could eat corn out of his pocket. The smaller birds crowded around and Tatu threw some corn on the ground and fed the little ones out of his hand. There was a waddling flock of marreca ducks, pretty little wild things not much bigger than pigeons. They looked as if they had been painted with bronze paint.

A rhea bird towered over all the rest, for he is a kind of small ostrich and has very long legs. There were some doves, too, that kept cooing.

Meanwhile Pepe and Nene were much excited and making a great racket, asking for corn. José spread some grains on the porch rail and broke them with a stone until they were the right size for the parakeets' small bills. Then he held out his forefingers, and they stepped on to be carried to the porch railing.

They were all enjoying themselves very much when Perla and Boy suddenly appeared. They had heard the noise and came squawking at the top of their parrot voices. Of course they were not hungry, for they always had plenty of their own corn in the feed box of their perch. But they were afraid they were missing something. They marched around proudly showing off before the other birds, for they were the favorite pets. Weren't they allowed to live on the front veranda where the family sat? And weren't they permitted even to come to the table sometimes when the grownups were through, to eat fruit and drink out of the children's cups? Perla and Boy evidently felt very superior. And for that reason José would not give them any corn at first. He made them wait until the others had eaten quite a lot. That quieted them down quickly enough.

Pretty soon Bill, the tame toucan, came paddling across the lot behind his great beak. He could not walk fast in flat places, because he was used to spending his time climbing trees looking for bugs in the hollows and peering under leaves for his dinner. By the time he arrived all the corn was gone, and José had to go back to the basket for more.

And then Perla spied the two new parakeets, nibbling cracked corn on the railing. In a minute she was climbing up beside them, very excited again. But this time she was gurgling and bubbling, seeming to tell Pepe and Nene that she thought they were little darlings. She did not frighten them, but sidled along the rail slowly, putting her head first to one side and then to the other to take a good look at them. When she was quite near she sat still, and swayed from side to side, making those gurgling friendly noises.

Pepe and Nene went on eating. They did not pay any attention, so she went closer and held out one claw as if to shake hands. When the parakeets did not move away, she stroked Pepe with her claw, which was almost as big as he was. Then she held onto him gently and began to smooth his feathers with her bill. Pepe liked that at first, for his feathers were a bit rumpled from the morning's adventures. But when he grew tired of it and tried to get away, he could not move. Perla held him tight. He wriggled and squirmed, roughing up all the feathers Perla had just made so tidy. He was a strong little bird and it was all Perla could do to hold him, so she laid him down on the rail and stood on him, while he squawked and cried. And Nene looked on out of one eye, not knowing what to do.

José came to the rescue, scolding Perla and flipping at her bill with his thumb and finger until she let go. Pepe shook himself, walked out of reach, and started to straighten out his feathers again.

But now came Nene's turn, for Perla was not at all discouraged. She chuckled and held Nene close while she petted and smoothed her. Nene stayed very quiet, enjoying all this attention, while the boys watched.

"You know," said Tatu. "I think Perla imagines she is Nene's mother."

"I think so, too," said José. "That is the way mother parrots take care of their babies. Perla has no babies of her own and she thinks Pepe and Nene are young because they are so little."

"I guess she has adopted them," Tatu agreed.

"If she really has adopted them," José went on, "they are in for a lot of care. Just you watch after today, and I'll bet you'll see Perla coming to see that they wash their hands and faces and brush their teeth!"

José was right, and after that Tatu did see Perla come each day to the porch rail where Pepe and Nene had made themselves at home. The other rail belonged to Guapo (meaning handsome), the gray monkey, so called because of his elegant fur. Perla would come and run her bill down each parakeet's feathers until they shone and not a speck of dust could be seen on them anywhere.

But now Tatu was anxious to examine all the creatures peeking out from the dozens of pens and cages out here among the trees and shrubs. He turned to fill his pockets again with corn.

"Oh, let's take the whole basket!" said José.

In the first pen was a capivara, a bristly-haired brown animal as big as a pig, but shaped like a guinea pig. His name was Cap. He was very tame, and he wanted to have his back scratched and his ears rubbed. José said a hunter had captured him at a pond in the forest and brought him back alive. The family bought him thinking what a fine meal he would make for everybody, for he was so nice and fat. But they waited a few days for someone's birthday which would mean a feast. Meanwhile Cap had become so friendly that no one had had the heart to kill him, let alone eat him. So here he was, the most amusing pet in the orchard. He ate corn out of Tatu's hand, taking it carefully, for his teeth were very long and sharp, and worked in his mouth like a pair of scissors. When José opened the small gate of his pen and let Cap out, he went straight over to the wash tank and climbed in for a bath, for capivaras love the water.

The next big cage was made of chicken wire, and in it was a pair of red-brown squirrels who whirled on a wheel and swung on their trapeze. They put on quite a show, because of the reward of corn they could smell.

Half a dozen jabotis were patiently waiting in another pen for the day to come when they would become jaboti stew. Tatu peered over their fence and they raised up their turtle heads to see what he was bringing them. Jabotis are land tortoises with pretty shells and vermilion-spotted legs.

"What they like is lettuce," said José. So he cut some from the platform vegetable garden. And they went into it like rabbits.

The rest of the pens were full of domestic animals and chickens. In one was a mother pig with nine little ones.

And now they were at the far end of the quintal, which is the word for orchard in the Portuguese language. Here was a big shelter made of palm leaves with a palm-leaf roof. Underneath, in the shade, stood Jasmina, and, beside her, Tatu saw a bigger horse, all white, with shining white mane and tail. Fastened to its bridle was a piece of paper with writing on it. Tatu read:

"Dear Mr. Amaral: My name is Branquissimo (whitest). And I hope your little boy likes me."

It was a wonderful name, for surely this was the whitest horse in the world.

Branquissimo, sniffing the corn, whinnied softly and stuck out his nose. It was like velvet. Tatu held up the basket. He and his new horse were friends at once.

Meanwhile Jasmina was whinnying, too, wondering why she was neglected. So Tatu emptied some of the corn into her manger and gave her a pat.

Just then Mamai's voice came floating out from the porch. "Tatu! Where are you?"

"Here!" he called back.

"Why don't you come in and take your siesta?" She sounded a little cross again. He knew he had to go. Only stopping to empty the basket into Branquissimo's manger, he trotted back to the house, José beside him.

Mamai was there, with Sr. Diogo.

The minute Sr. Diogo saw the basket dangling empty from José's arm, he looked very serious.

"What have you done with the corn?" he asked.

"We fed the animals, Grandfather," answered José, looking worried.

"You know the cook shelled enough corn for two days, and now you have given it to them all at once," said Sr. Diogo, severely. "What are they going to eat tomorrow? And what will Sr. Amaral say when he sees it's all gone?"

"It was my fault," said Tatu, for he did not want José to be blamed. "José did it for me to get acquainted."

"Never mind, Sr. Diogo," Mamai interrupted. "I will speak to Sr. Amaral and explain about the corn. And now, Tatu, into your hammock."

Tatu was not feeling a bit sleepy. Neither was José, who said he had something else to do.

"Look, José! We are the only people awake," said Tatu.

He pointed out the quintal with a large sweep of his arm. All the creatures were quiet as mice, well fed and sleepy. And on the porch railing Perla was nodding. Under the edge of her feathers were Pepe and Nene, cuddling like baby chickens.

"Into your hammocks, both of you," said Mamai. "And, Tatu, don't you wake up Joa by squeaking too loudly."

V

Tatu Loses a Letter

RIDING INTO TOWN one day on Jasmina and Branquissimo, the two Amaral children saw a lot of busyness that seemed to tell them something was about to happen. In the houses the women were sitting before their doors working on their sewing machines. The stores were busy, too, with many customers leaning over the counters. They could see clerks reeling off yards and yards of goods. They were holding up pieces of sateen and silk to show the bright colors. In the streets and resting in the praça, the park in front of the cathedral, were crowds of country people.

Tatu and Joa had some money which Mamai had given them for ices, so they got off their horses at the Mascotte and sat down at a table. All the other tables were full, and here on the terrace they saw a lot of children they'd never seen before. And they were all talking about the Christmas festival.

It was pleasant on the terrace of the Mascotte that overhangs the beach where, as usual, there were lots of people. Some had come down to bathe in the river, for everyone in Santarem likes to take a bath twice a day. Others were car-

rying water to their kitchens at home in two big square gaso-
line tins, fitted with handles and balanced on both ends of a
pole across their shoulders.

Water for cooking and drinking is brought from the middle
of the river by canoes, because it is pure out there. And this
morning quite a few canoes were coming toward shore loaded
with water cans. After it has been filtered, it is fine to drink.
But water from shore is good enough for cleaning and for
washing.

All day long the boys and men come from the beach with

their double loads and carry them to all the families in town. That is the way they make their living.

Tatu and Joa could see the wharf from their table at the Mascotte. A big steamer was being loaded. Men were running across her gangplank, carrying sacks of corn and rice and bales of cotton, on their heads. Near by, fishermen, wading in the water, were throwing their round nets into the shallow edges of the river. Every time the nets were pulled in and opened on the sand, Tatu could see fish jumping.

It was very nice there, sitting under the jasmine arbor that smelled so sweet, with the cool morning wind blowing up the river. Joa had ordered an ice made of custard apple. And Tatu was eating pineapple sherbet. They were very good.

But soon their ices were gone, and the children were up on Jasmina and Branquissimo, clattering down the street again. Mamai had told them to stop at the post office and see if there were any letters. Joa waited outside on Jasmina and held Branquissimo's reins while Tatu went inside. He came out with a letter. It was from their big brothers at home on the plantation. But it was addressed to Papai and Mamai, so Tatu didn't open it.

There was just one more errand to do. They had to call at a pillow-lace-maker's house to ask if she had finished some lace for Mamai to sew on Joa's new dress. This time Joa dismounted, too, for she wanted to look at the lace. Unfortunately it was not quite done. But the lace-maker was trying hard to finish it that afternoon, she said.

The pillow she worked on was propped up on a table in front of her. It was shaped like a cylinder and looked like an old-fashioned bed bolster. It was stuck full of pins, arranged in a pattern. The threads were on separate bobbins. The lace-maker threw a bobbin in such a way that its thread caught over a pin. Then she threw another so its thread caught over a different pin. And so on until every pin was holding a thread and one could see exactly how the design worked out. But the woman worked so fast that neither Tatu nor Joa could keep track of the threads as they caught on the pins. Besides there were so many bobbins it was a wonder she could tell one from the other. They simply flew through the air. And they made a pretty clicking noise, for each one had a hollow tucum seed on the end, which made it look like a small baby's rattle with thread wound around the handle.

Tatu was trying to count the bobbins, but he gave it up. The lace-maker told him there were thirty altogether. But she knew how to make lace with fifty. And that was very difficult indeed, for even she became confused, sometimes, and had to undo some of the pattern when she made a mistake. Joa thought she could stay there all day watching until her lace was all ready. It was so pretty. And the lace-maker's fingers were so nimble. But Tatu kept nudging her until finally Joa said to please excuse them, they had to go.

"Why did you want to stay so long in there?" Tatu asked his sister crossly.

"You liked it, too, at first anyway," Joa answered.

"Well, I wanted to understand how she did it. But that didn't take me forever," Tatu complained. "I don't like lace."

"You would if you could wear some on your shirt," said Joa. She thought she had got the better of the argument, for Tatu had nothing more to say.

He started to help her mount. The curbstone was very high and Jasmina was very short. But Joa could reach the stirrup easily and sprang up by herself, quite triumphant.

Just at that moment a piano started playing in a house across the street. There were the opening bars of a song. And then a lot of children voices piped up. It was quite pretty and Tatu and Joa both were very still, listening. So many children sounded like a school. This was vacation time, though. They were wondering what it could be, when a lady appeared at the door. She came right up to Joa, sitting there on Jasmina.

"Aren't you Sra. Amaral's little girl?" she asked.

"Yes, Senhora. I am Joa."

"Well, isn't this fortunate! We have a number of girls practicing pastorals for Christmas. Wouldn't you like to join them?"

Joa thought she should ask Mamai. But she didn't have time to say that, for the lady went on: "I have met your mother. And I am sure she will like to have you with us. Tell her I am Dona Josefina."

"How long will it take?" asked Tatu.

"Just an hour," answered Dona Josefina.

"Go on, Joa," said Tatu. And that settled it.

So Joa climbed down out of the saddle. And Tatu said he would come back for her in an hour. He dropped the reins over Jasmina's head so she would step on them if she tried to walk, and told her to stay by the curb until he came back. Then he jumped on Branquissimo who paced down the street doing his best gaits. Tatu didn't know what to do now. He would ride through the main street first. Then perhaps he would go back to the Mascotte and have another ice.

When he came to the market the whole open space between it and the beach was full of people. Fishermen had arrived in their boats. Sails were flapping loose. The bright colors were lovely in the sun. Blue and red and brown sails are much prettier than plain white ones—and those are the colors fishermen like. Their fish were laid out on tables along the beach below the market.

A farmer had brought his calf for sale and it was standing in his dugout waiting for a customer. Other boats were full of melons and great yellow pumpkins. Still others were unloading pigs and goats, chickens and turkeys. Women were hurrying down with their baskets to get the best bargains. And Tatu could see that all the stalls inside the market building were busy.

He and Branquissimo stopped on the paved street above, to watch all this. And as they stood there, by the stairs leading down to the beach, who should come paddling along in their canoe but Sr. Diogo and José. They were looking for an opening where they could land. Pretty soon they found one between two bigger boats. They dragged the canoe up on shore and walked past the fishermen's tables. When they started for the stairs they spied Tatu.

"Hello, Tatu! What are you doing here?" asked Sr. Diogo.

"Nothing," he answered. "Joa is practicing for the festival and I'm just waiting for her."

"Well, that's fine," said Sr. Diogo. "José hasn't anything to do either while I look after my business. So you can amuse each other."

José looked pleased at that.

"Now you two boys run along and have a good time for an hour," Sr. Diogo smiled.

"Where'll I meet you?" asked José.

"Can't he come home with me?" Tatu suggested.

"Yes, may I?" urged José.

"I guess I can get along without you. In fact I won't have to do much paddling going down with the current." Sr. Diogo held out his hand for José's foot and gave him a lift up behind Tatu.

"Thank you, Grandpa," said José.

"There is one thing I will let you do for me," Sr. Diogo said.

"What's that?" asked Tatu.

"Your mother wants some ice for lunch. You can stop for it at the Mascotte on the way home. Now, don't forget. And don't be late, because she's counting on that ice to make cool drinks."

They promised they would get the ice and wouldn't be late. Sr. Diogo gave Branquissimo a little slap on his rump that sent him off in fine style.

"What'll we do?" Tatu asked, over his shoulder.

"Let's go over to the Indian village and look for relics," suggested José.

Tatu had heard about these pottery heads and animals that had been buried in the ground since before Columbus came to America. They were something like the pumice stone head he had found in front of his house.

"How do we get there?" Tatu asked eagerly.

"It's only a little way beyond the praça," José explained. "We can be there in five minutes."

Tatu guided Branquissimo past the cathedral and on past a few houses with thick walls painted pink and blue and yellow. They went by the electric light plant where a big boat was unloading wood to burn for running the dynamos. And then they came to houses made of palm leaves, with palm-leaf roofs. This was the aldeia, as an Indian village is called. Except there were no longer any real Indians here. They had had their own civilization years and years ago. Now one could scarcely tell the difference between them and anyone else in Santarem.

"Let's stop here," said José suddenly.

Tatu reined in Branquissimo and they both slid to the ground.

"I once found a clay alligator here and the head of an Indian idol. But it was after a big rain had washed them out," said José. He took a stick and began to turn over small stones and dig in the soft dirt. Tatu found a stick and did the same, but as yet he didn't know what to hunt for.

Pretty soon Tatu turned up a bit of red pottery that looked interesting. But José told him it was only a piece of somebody's broken cooking pot. The minutes flew. The boys worked steadily.

"Oh, look!" exclaimed José. He was quite excited, digging furiously around the edges of something large and red. Tatu helped and after awhile they had uncovered enough to show what it was.

"Just the rest of your old broken cook pot," José decided. He was quite disgusted.

By this time a number of people were passing them, going back to town, or coming home to the aldeia. Tatu had forgotten all about Joa, and now he suddenly remembered.

"José! What time is it?" he exclaimed, for José could tell time by the sun.

José didn't look up at the sun, however. He looked down at his shadow instead, which at this minute was growing very short indeed.

"It is half past eleven already."

"Joa's hour is up. We'll have to hurry," said Tatu.

José climbed into the saddle, Tatu jumped up in front of him and Branquissimo seemed to know all about it for he broke into a gallop that took them through the town in a hurry. There shopkeepers were taking some of their goods down from the doorways. They were getting ready to close for their noon meal and siesta.

In no time the boys were in the street of the lace-maker. The girls were just coming out of Dona Josefina's house. And there was Joa with a paper in her hand. She said hello, then asked Tatu to put the paper in his pocket, for on it were the words of a song she had to learn. That reminded Tatu of the letter they had gotten at the post office. He felt for it and it wasn't there. The letter from the big brothers at home, that Mamai and Papai had been expecting, was gone!

Dona Josefina came out and offered to help Joa up. But Joa managed by herself. And then Tatu had to confess that he had lost the letter. What would he do?

"It probably fell out of your pocket while you were stooping over, looking for relics," suggested José. "We might be able to find it."

"Maybe—" said Tatu doubtfully.

He turned Branquissimo's head toward the aldeia again.

But this time they rode very slowly, looking in the street and along the gutters. When they got back to the spot where they had been digging they couldn't see it there either. But the boys picked up their sticks again and poked the ground.

"Here it is!" exclaimed Tatu, pushing away the earth where they had discovered the cooking pot. The letter had fallen and they had completely covered it without even noticing.

Tatu brushed off the dirt and the envelope looked quite clean. He was so glad, and kept thinking about it all the way back through the town, and so did José.

"My, I'm thirsty," Joa complained. "I wish I had a sherbet —ice—or even a drink."

"The ice!" Tatu almost shouted.

And José struck his forehead with his hand. They had completely forgotten about Mamai's ice and had ridden right past the Mascotte. How could they have been so thoughtless when his grandfather had made them promise!

Again Tatu turned Branquissimo around.

"Where are you going?" Joa wanted to know.

"Back to the Mascotte!" Tatu replied.

"Oh, goody, goody!" cried Joa. "Now I can have an ice! I'm going to order pineapple this time."

But when they got to the Mascotte, Tatu spoke to her very positively.

"You stay here, Joa," he said, in his most bossy way.

"What for?" asked Joa.

But Tatu didn't even hear. He ran in and rushed out again, carrying a little newspaper package that showed bits of sawdust at the ends. And away they rode at a gallop to keep the ice from melting, Branquissimo ahead and Jasmina close behind.

Joa didn't even have a chance to say how mean she thought Tatu was, nor how hot and thirsty and cross she felt. All she could do was to hold on to Jasmina's reins and guide her.

José was carrying the ice. The sun was very hot now. And the ice was melting fast. Cold water dripped out of the package and splashed on the back of Tatu's shirt. Soon he was quite wet, but it felt nice because he was so hot.

When they came near the house the front porch was empty. Mamai and Papai were sitting at the table on the side veranda. And Maria was bringing a tureen of soup from the kitchen.

"Just in time!" said Papai.

But Mamai did not say anything. She only invited José to lunch. Then she handed Maria the ice and told her to break it up and put it in the glasses. And to bring the pitcher of refresco, fresh fruit juice mixed with water.

Tatu had scarcely lifted his soup spoon to his mouth before Mamai asked him what was that spot on his shoulder. She made him turn around and show his wet back. Then of course he had to go into the hammock room and change his shirt. For he would surely catch cold sitting in the wind that way.

Meanwhile, Joa was doing enough talking for all of them, telling how Dona Josefina had invited her to take part in the pastorals. She would have to learn the songs, and go to practice every morning. And if she did very well, Dona Josefina had said she could sing a solo verse all by herself. She didn't know what part she would take yet. Dona Josefina would decide that later. But the most important point of all to Joa was the costume. Would Mamai make her one?

Mamai said, "Yes, of course." And Joa's face shone.

"But you will have to tell me what to make pretty soon," Mamai smiled.

"I think I'd like to be an angel," Joa said thoughtfully.

"That would be very appropriate," remarked Papai, his eyes twinkling.

Tatu came back holding out the letter that he had forgotten again. And Papai read it aloud while waiting for Maria to bring something more to eat.

The letter was full of good news from home, far away in the State of Río de Janeiro. The rains had been just right. The coffee was heavy on the trees, the sugar cane was tall and juicy, and all the fruits were wonderful this year. Everybody was well, and the big sisters were still visiting their aunts and uncles in the Capital. They were going to be very citified when they came home.

Cavalette, the little black and white horse, was growing too fat and frisky without any children to ride him. Sentinel, the great yellow dog, at last had stopped searching for them all over the house. And Jacá, the brown monkey, and Louro, the yellow-headed parrot, were lonely. They sent their love, and wanted to know when Tatu and Joa were coming home. The big brothers were lonely, too. They especially missed their little brother's and sister's noise and liveliness.

"When are you all coming back?" they asked at the end of the letter.

"When are we?" Tatu asked. He felt a little homesick, thinking of his brothers and sisters and all the pets left behind.

"When my work here is done, Son," Papai replied thoughtfully. And then he smiled. "I'll let you know in plenty of time to pack all your things."

This reminded Tatu of the aldeia. And he told how he and José had hunted for Indian relics.

"I think we had better take care of the junk you already have, instead of your getting any more," said Mamai. "It is scattered around everywhere."

"Maybe we can find Tatu a table and a cabinet and let him start a museum, Mamai," suggested Papai.

"Of course we can. That's a good idea," said Mamai.

VI

Peixe-Boi Goes to the Party

TATU WAS ARRANGING his museum, and Joa was helping him.

Mamai had given him a long narrow table against the living-room wall. She had put the bookcase alongside. And she said he could have three shelves behind the glass doors. Then his best exhibits would not get broken or dusty.

Several of his finest things were broken already. They had been packed and unpacked so many times. So many people had looked at and handled them. But he had Scotch tape, the paste jar, and the glue tube from Papai's traveling office outfit. And now Joa was holding two pieces of a broken butterfly wing together on the table. Tatu cut a bit of Scotch tape just the right size. He laid it on the broken wing. When they turned the butterfly over, it was as good as ever. Joa glued back the legs of a number of bugs that had been nearly worn out, and the head of a big beetle that looked like a rhinoceros.

When all the insects were fixed, Tatu mounted them. First he spread a layer of cotton in a frame. He arranged all the butterflies on the cotton, with a big blue one in the middle.

Some of the butterflies had streaks of real gold and real silver on their wings. Tatu put these around the blue one. Then he made a pattern with the others. He had all the colors of the rainbow, yellow, orange, red, violet, blue and green. Besides, there were black ones with red and green stripes, and brown ones with orange spots.

When he was through, Joa said they looked beautiful. And she helped him fasten each one firmly with a pin that stuck through the cotton into the wood underneath.

The bugs went into another frame. The big rhinoceros beetle made a nice center piece. He surely was ugly. But so many Brazilian beetles are gilded with green and bronze and gold, that, after all, the bug frame was nearly as pretty as the one with the butterflies. Tatu set the frames up side by side on the top shelf. He laid his Indian necklace in front of them. It was made of green-gilt beetle wings and black beetle heads.

Then came his three tatus or armadillos, which he collected because Tatu was his nickname. His real name was Manoel Octavio da Silva Amaral.

There was a stuffed baby tatu that had once been alive. It was pink and the size of a chipmunk. A small brown one was made of guarana paste. It could be grated and used for making guarana tea. But Tatu thought it was too pretty to spoil just for a drink. The third was a little pottery bank in the shape of an armadillo. It had a slit in the top for dropping in coins. If he ever used it to save his money he would have to break it open to get the coins out. It was already broken a little, though. The end of its tail had come off. Joa said she could mend it. But first she shook it to make sure there was no money inside. She glued the tail and fastened it with a bit of Scotch tape until the glue could dry. Then she set the tatus up, one after the other, a little procession of armadillos on the shelf.

It was fun, for Joa had clever fingers. And she was working so hard that Tatu suddenly remembered that she had an interesting collection, too.

"Wouldn't you like a shelf for your dolls, Sister?" he suggested.

"Are you sure you can spare one?" she asked.

"Of course I can," said Tatu. "Besides there's going to be lots of room on the table. I'll arrange my birds' nests on the second shelf, and you can have the third."

"That will be wonderful," Joa exclaimed.

"We can put your name on the shelf, and we'll make a label for each doll—where it came from and what it represents," Tatu suggested.

"Oh, Tatu! It'll be like a real museum!" Joa's eyes were shining.

She ran to unpack her dolls which were still in her suitcase. She had forgotten how nice they were. And how long she had neglected them. There was Bina, the black doll she had gotten in Bahia, with embroidered white teeth and pretty smile. She had real fingernails, too, cut out of the quills of chicken feathers and fastened into her cloth fingers. Joa shook out her full flowered skirts and ruffled petticoats, straightened her plaid shawl, glass bead necklaces, and the basket of fruit on her head. And then she gave Bina a real hug, for she was very fond of her Bahian doll.

She gathered up an armful of Indians with parrot feather headdresses, and hurried back to the living room.

Her brother was busy lettering her name, all of it, for Joa was just part of her first name. "Joaquina Maria Antonia da Silva Amaral," he wrote on a card. He had to fill two lines because her name was so long.

While Joa made the dolls feel at home on their shelf, Tatu went on making labels, doing his best writing. Every once in a while he asked a question.

"What's the name of this Indian with the feather skirt and crown, and with a silver snake in her hand?"

"She's a princess. So I call her Tuchawa. That's Indian for chief or queen."

"I know," said Tatu, writing it down. "And who is the other fine Indian with the big necklace and the bow and arrow?"

"He's a prince. But he hasn't any name yet," answered Joa.

"Let's call him Guarany, after the Indian prince in the opera, Guarany," suggested Tatu.

"I like that," agreed Joa.

"And the others?" Tatu asked again.

"Oh, I don't know any more names. Let's just call them Indians." So Tatu wrote, "Indian warrior dolls made of canaraná pith by Amazon Indians, and dyed with colors out of the forest."

When Mamai came to see how they were getting along, the museum was nearly ready. Tatu was just laying out the last things on the table—painted gourds with river scenes on them, and some pretty painted river stones showing herons standing in the water. He added his pumice stone head and his alligator-tooth charm, said to keep snakes away . . . though, of course, he didn't believe that.

"I don't know what to do with these." He stopped to think as Mamai arrived. He was holding up two dusters of macaw feathers.

"I'll show you," said his mother.

She placed a duster at each corner of the bookcase top. And then she stood back to see the effect. They looked like flames of fire shooting upward.

"Oh, I like them that way!" Joa clapped her hands.

Tatu agreed that Mamai had added just the right finishing touch. And his mother was pleased.

"And now you have company, so come on outside," Mamai said. "Maria's brother and sister have come to see you."

The sister's name was Sara. She was ten years old. And the brother's name was Tomás. He was nine, just Joa's age. But he was as tall as his sister, nearly as big as Tatu.

Maria introduced them. Then she went on with her washing. She had the biggest tin washbasin you ever saw. It was full of water from the river and she sat on a high log in the dry sand of the beach, soaping the clothes in the basin. She did a few at a time, rubbed them with her hands, and rinsed them in the river. The green water was in, and Maria said she liked to see the garments come out of the river all clean. It was nice to hang them on the line in the sun afterward and have them flutter in the breeze like a lot of banners.

The children watched her while getting acquainted.

Near by was Sr. Diogo, who was building a bathhouse on the beach. Its skeleton was already done. He had driven poles deep into the sand and had nailed on the crosspieces and roof poles. A place was left for a door, and there was a board floor, but no window. Beside him was a pile of dried palm leaves. They were the kind that look like huge feathers. When he took his knife and sliced off one side of a leaf, it was like fringe. He was making all the leaves into fringe, now, as he called out, "Good afternoon, children!"

They all said "Good afternoon, Sr. Diogo." And then they asked Maria to please excuse them, for what Sr. Diogo was doing looked much more interesting than washing clothes.

Sr. Diogo was all ready to thatch the bath-house. He tacked up a row of palm fringe that swept the sand all around it. The second row went on a little farther up, so it fell over the first row. The third row followed, a few inches higher still. And so on, each row overlapping the one below it. Sr. Diogo worked so fast that the skeleton was looking like a house already—or rather, like a play house. When finished, there would be room inside for a big tin basin, like Maria's, full of water. And space beside the basin for a person to undress, hang up his clothes on pegs, and take a "gourd bath." This is very refreshing when the yellow water is in, and sting rays might be lurking in the murky river bed. Besides, it is the only way to get a soap bath. After a good wetting with a gourd full of water, and a thorough soaping, the big gourd goes to the basin again and again, and the bather empties it over himself until all the soap is washed away. The soapy water runs down through the floor cracks into the sand.

Sr. Diogo said he would soon have the walls and roof all thatched. Tatu and Joa could have baths inside that very evening if they wished. They said that would be fun.

"What will we use for a door?" asked Joa.

"I have it already made, Joa. Look!" Sr. Diogo laid down his hammer and pushed aside the pile of palm fringes. Underneath was a woven palm-leaf mat, just the size to cover the door frame.

"After you go inside, hang up the mat, and you couldn't have a better door," explained Sr. Diogo.

Joa thought that a very clever idea. Altogether the bath-house was going to be perfect.

"And now," Tatu said to the guests, seeing that bath-houses were an old story to them, "how would you like to look at our museum?"

Sara and Tomás thought that would be nice. They were dressed up for their first visit, and looked very fine in their white clothes and white shoes. Their hair was combed smooth and shiny, and black as night, like their big eyes. But they felt a little shy with such traveled children as Tatu and Joa. When they saw the museum, though, they were right at home. For here were things they knew about, even better than Tatu himself.

Pretty soon, Mamai called to them from the veranda. She had set crackers and cakes and buttered rolls on the table. Now she was pouring maté (tea) into their cups, and laying a cut lime on each saucer to squeeze into it. While the children were sitting down, along came Sr. Diogo who had finished his work on the bath-house.

"Where is José?" Mamai inquired.

"I told him to mind the calves until I came back," said Sr. Diogo. "Do you need him for something?"

"Indeed I do," Mamai smiled. "I need another boy to help eat up these cakes. Can you spare him?"

They felt a little shy with such traveled children as Tatu and Joa

"Thank you for the invitation. I'll send him right over."

Mamai went for another plate and cup and saucer, and José came running.

Things were more lively now for José was an old friend of Tomás and Sara. And they had so many jokes together that no one noticed Peixe-Boi, the great black bull, ambling across the sands slowly toward the veranda. When he heard the fun he wanted to be in it. He walked up close and looked on, very much interested. When the children paid no attention to him, he soon grew tired of being left out of the party. So he gave a great snort, and pawed the loose dirt with his front hoof until it flew through the air all over the porch floor. The dust flew everywhere. It was thick and suffocating. Mamai began to cough. She ran to the edge of the veranda, waved her hands and shouted, "Shoo! Shoo! Go away, you big beast!"

That was just what Peixe-Boi wanted—a little attention. He looked at her with mischief in his eyes, and started to paw up the dust again, glancing up to see the effect on Mamai.

But José knew what to do. He jumped off the veranda, seized a little switch that happened to be lying there, and struck Peixe-Boi across his black face. The bull lowered his horns, and Mamai screamed. She was sure he was going to hook José. But the weak little switch was broken already. It could not have hurt. Only Peixe-Boi's feelings were very much hurt. He backed away, and stood looking at them mournfully.

"Poor Peixe-Boi!" Joa mourned with him. "He can't help it because he is so huge and clumsy. He wants to play with us."

"Let's give him a cake," said Tatu, feeling as sorry as Joa.

Peixe-Boi ran out his long tongue and licked the cake from Tatu's hand. After this great treat Peixe-Boi waddled on up the beach. All was forgiven. Awhile later Boneca came to the bars. She felt she was the favorite cow and should have anything good that was being handed out. So Joa took Boneca a cake and when she fed it to her, Boneca's tongue felt like a tin grater.

"That's all right," said Maria, coming back from washing. "But what if Peixe-Boi thinks he is rewarded for being bad, and does it again the next time he wants cake?"

Then the black bull was forgotten while the children ate their own cakes. But he was not going to stay out of the limelight long. There was a sound of crashing wood on the beach. And there lay the new bath-house, all smashed flat! Peixe-Boi stood over it, sniffing the wreck and wondering how he could have pushed it over so easily. He knew he would surely be in disgrace now, and looked around for something pleasing that human beings might like. Ah, he had it! Maria's washing was waving to him on the line. In a minute he had hooked off a pink skirt of Joa's on one horn, and Tatu's blue shorts on the other. He was all dressed up now, and the people would surely admire him. So he made a one-bull parade of himself, walking proudly with his new decorations. There was a good audience on the veranda this time, including Sr. Diogo whose hard work on the bath-house was now all lost.

Maria rushed out to rescue the clothes from being torn by the bull's sharp horns. The skirt and shorts would have to be washed over again. So this time Sr. Diogo snapped a lead strap into the ring in Peixe-Boi's nose, led him away to the solitary confinement corral, and shut him in.

And next morning Peixe-Boi was still there, looking out and pretending to be sorry, although the bars were down. Sr. Diogo wondered how that had happened.

Many people had seen the big black animal during the night, walking all around the town. So they kept saying to Sr. Diogo, thinking it was a good joke,

"What was your bull doing, taking a promenade all by himself last night? We'd think a careful man like you would keep your valuable animals safely shut up."

Peixe-Boi had learned to let the bars down, but he didn't know how to put them up again.

VII

Joa Is an Angel

JOA WAS VERY BUSY, for every morning she went to Dona Josefina's house to practice with twenty other girls. Several of the taller ones (about Tatu's size) took the principal parts in the pastorals. Most of the girls were Joa's age, however, so she was making many new friends.

Papai had decided that Joa and Jasmina could be trusted to ride into town by themselves now, so Tatu didn't have to go with her any more. It was really only a short distance to town and Jasmina was such a good little horse. Mamai said it was all right with her if Joa was to ride in alone, if only she would be sure to come home to lunch on time. Doing that proved to be a hard task later on, for when the practicing was over Dona Josefina always made things especially interesting for Joa and the others.

She had made Joa's wish come true by giving her the part of an angel in the pastorals. And Joa was very happy when she saw the yards of gauze that Mamai had bought and started to sew for her costume. She had ordered wings made of real feathers, too. It was hard to wait now for the time to come.

But Dona Josefina's fascinating stories helped to make the

time pass more quickly. Sometimes she played for them, too, and then told them about the music. Other times she accompanied them on the piano while they played games, even old ones like ring-around-the-rosie that were fun when they all took part. The one they all liked best was about a stone wall. Dona Josefina said that this game was very old, too, and that children were playing it in Portugal long before de Cabral discovered Brazil.

When Joa was wearing her dress with the very full skirt she was chosen to be "It," and then picked out five girls to play with her. They stood in a circle with Joa in the middle, all of them facing her. Each of the five girls reached out her right hand and took hold of the hem of Joa's dress, making her full skirt stand out perfectly flat around her, like a table.

At that point Joa was a prisoner, and the five girls her prison wall. Then they were ready to begin the game. The girls, including Joa, started to sing and Dona Josefina played the tune that went like this:

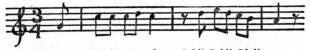

Come see the dungeon keep O-lé! O-lé! Ol-é!
One stone I'll just knock down O-lé! O-lé! O-lé!

But the wall is very steep O-lé! O-lé! O-lé!
No matter if one is gone O-lé! O-lé! O-lé!

The song had five verses, all sung exactly the same way. They sang the first two lines—

> "Come see the dungeon keep. O-lé! O-lé! O-lé!
> But the wall is very steep. O-lé! O-lé! O-lé!"

Then when they came to the third line—

> "One stone I'll just knock down. O-lé! O-lé! O-lé!"

Joa did just what the song said. She knocked down one of the hands holding her skirt. That girl was then "out" and left the ring. Then the others finished singing the last line—

> "No matter if one is gone. O-lé! O-lé! O-lé!"

And then they would begin the song all over again, and put the second girl "out." Repeating, they would put the third girl "out," repeat and put the fourth girl "out." When only one girl was left of the original five, she walked around the empty circle, holding up one corner of Joa's dress while Joa turned with her. When Joa had knocked down the last hand, the last stone had fallen. There was no more wall, and then Joa was free.

The girl who was the last stone then became the one who was "It." Whereupon, the game would begin all over again. Joa was sure that it was her favorite game.

Meanwhile Christmas was coming nearer and nearer. But that did not mean a lot of gifts, for the day when Brazilian children receive most of their presents is the sixth of January. This is called the Day of the Kings, and celebrates the arrival of the three kings at the manger. They have traveled far across the desert, following the Star of Bethlehem and bringing rich gifts to the Christ-child. Christmas Day is a fine holiday, though, with a big dinner, many parties and, perhaps, a present or two for each child as a promise of what they will receive two weeks later.

In every kitchen special cooking was going on. All over town the air was perfumed with vanilla and caramel, with the smell of cakes baking and sugar boiling.

Several days before Christmas Alzira was working from morning until night. She was grinding spices with her mortar and pestle, and cutting up candied fruits, and shelling peanuts. As soon as she would get a batch of kisses done and dropped into their pans, Maria would run with it to the house of a neighbor. This woman had a big outdoor oven made of stones plastered with clay. And she did the baking for the entire neighborhood. There were dreams, and almond cakes, and decorated cookies, all being guarded against the ants in big tin boxes on the kitchen shelves. But Alzira said that boys were much more destructive than ants. For Tatu and José hung about the door like a pair of beggars. And Alzira could not resist the big hungry eyes they made. She kept going to a tin box and robbing it of a few cookies at a time.

Finally she said if they wanted to eat they would have to work. She was about to make bola de macacheira, which is a special Christmas treat like both a pudding and a cake. They could help her very much if they would grate the coconut and the macacheira root.

José said he had to let the calves out for their run. Alzira answered that it was funny he had not thought about that before.

It was true, though. He had forgotten all about the calves, thinking about Alzira's good cookies. And now he and Tatu went to the corral and let down the bars. This was a part of José's work every day. But Tatu thought nearly all of José's work was like play.

The calves chased down the runway and out on the beach, with their big ears flopping and their tails flying. Bonequinho was in the lead as always. Boneca, his mother, was not acting at all like a "doll" now. She was leading the chorus of bawling cows, for she knew that her child was the worst of all when it came to running away.

There was not much chance of their running far today, though, for José and Tatu were in a hurry. They headed off the calves, turned them around, and in no time had them on the way back. This pleased the mothers, who started chewing their cuds, quite contented. But the calves couldn't understand why they were being cheated out of part of their fun. They poked along and refused to be hurried. Then Bonequinho decided he wanted a bath in the river. He skipped in until the water was up to his stomach. He refused to be coaxed out and José was just about to wade in after him, when Tatu said, "Wait a minute."

He ran into the house and came back with a cookie, which acted like magic. Bonequinho walked out of the river for it, and went back to the corral as meekly as the other calves.

Meanwhile Alzira had cracked the coconuts and saved the coconut milk. She peeled the brown skin off the white coconut meat, and the boys started grating. Alzira warned them to watch out and not grate their fingers.

Then she looked over her macacheira roots, which were brown, like potatoes, and almost as long as her arm. Macacheira is a kind of sweet mandioca. But it does not contain

poison, like the real mandioca which has to have special treat-
ment before it is fit to eat. She had to be careful that no real
mandioca was mixed in by mistake, for that would make
everybody very sick. It was easy for her to tell the difference,
but she wouldn't trust the boys to do this. She peeled the
roots she selected, and they were ready to grate when the
coconut was done. Then she mixed the grated root with the
grated coconut, beat in lots of eggs and sugar, and coconut
milk. She poured the batter into pans, with a special one for
José and Tatu as pay for their work. And Maria took them all
to the neighbor's oven.

Down in the town that same day a few families were
building a crèche, or manger, in their parlors. They made a
tiny, open, palm-thatched house, set toy palms and mango
trees around it, and laid out a walk with flower gardens. When
it was done it looked exactly like a real Amazon home. Inside the house they arranged miniature dolls for the Holy
Family, with the Baby in a crib under a drape of net. All the
animals were looking on—toy cows, donkeys, sheep and
goats, besides some pet wild animals and sometimes a camel.
And the smallest Christmas tree, hung with candles and
ornaments, shone down on everything. These crèches were
very pretty.

In Santarem, one of the principal Christmas events is the
singing of pastorales around these crèches, just as they were
sung in Portugal hundreds of years before the Portuguese
came to Brazil.

At last the important evening came. Joa had her supper
early, and rode down town before it was dark. Dona Josefina
needed plenty of time to see her troop nicely dressed. Besides,

she wanted to have them practice once more, singing with the violin, guitar and drum, instead of her piano.

Sr. Diogo piled the rest of the household into his canoe—Mamai, Papai, Tatu, Alzira, Maria, and José. He and Papai did the paddling. And that was the way they went to town. The canoe was a dugout, made of a hollowed log. It was very unsteady with the five grownups and two boys in it. The water came up almost to the very edge. Mamai kept saying that she was sure they would tip over, or that they would sink. When Tatu turned to tell her there was no danger, he rocked the boat the tiniest bit, and a little water came over the side. Mamai gasped. She was sure they were sinking. But José picked up a gourd and bailed the water out. Then he wiped the floor dry with a cloth so Mamai would not wet her shoes. He did all this without tilting the canoe at all, for he was used to balancing himself.

Papai said, "Now, Tatu, don't you dare move a finger. Don't even wink an eye, or you will have us all in the river." His voice sounded as if he were laughing. And then Mamai giggled a little, like Joa, and said she wouldn't be nervous any more.

It was a beautiful night. The full moon was making a silver path on the water. The houses of Santarem looked white as ghosts and the trees black as ink. Soon they came near the landing, and saw the cathedral outlined in electric lights for Christmas. Tatu said its two square towers with the cross between looked as if they were shining in the sky.

Joa's little audience landed from their canoe and lined up along the sidewalk where she was sure to pass. Other families were already there. Sara and Tomás came along and joined the Amarals, and soon there was a jolly crowd.

In a little while, the drum, violin and guitar could be heard, then the voices of the children singing. And the procession came in sight. After the musicians marched the heralds, two big girls in light blue satin tunics, and wide blue satin hats curled up at one side. They carried crooks, for they represented the shepherds that watched their flocks by night. Behind them floated Joa. At least she seemed to float. A silver crown was on her head, with gauze veils fluttering from it over her white dress. And through the veils peeked her snowy white wings of real feathers, fastened to her shoulders. She didn't look either to right or left, and neither did the others.

Then came more pastoral characters: carpenters, fishermen and farmers, and a lot of rough looking peasants. And at the very end, a Gypsy, shaking her tambourine hung with gay ribbons. That was all, except some of the spectators including the Amarals, who fell in behind. And this made quite a long procession.

The heralds led them to a house where there was a crèche. The doors were open, and the girls marched inside and surrounded the manger. They sang and danced before it. Then each good singer did her separate verse, all joining in the chorus. The verses told the story of the first Christmas. When Joa's turn came, she sang about how the angels guarded the Child from harm. Then there was a commotion outside, and a girl in costume rushed through the crowd in the street. She had got lost hunting for the manger. This was a part of the play. The other players hugged her and the drum beat a

loud tattoo. They led her up in front where she sang and danced by herself, while the violin and guitar played constantly.

When the story was nearly told, along came the Gypsy, rattling her tambourine, and singing, "Sou uma pobre Cigana. Dá-me esmola." "I am a poor Gypsy. Give me an offering." She came down the front steps and kept her song going while she passed the tambourine through the crowd. In no time at all it was rattling with coins to be given to charity.

And now the show was finished here. The girls marched out and the procession moved on to the next crèche, where they did it over again.

When all was ended, they were invited to Dona Josefina's

house, where she served ices and little cakes. Since the Amarals were strangers in Santarem, their party was invited, too. So that made a lovely end of the evening.

After they had said their good-bys and thanks to Dona Josefina, and complimented her and the girls on the fine show, they started home.

"We'll leave Jasmina at the Mascotte for the night, and Joa can come in the canoe with us," said Papai.

"Then we will surely sink!" exclaimed Mamai.

"Maybe you think Joa can fly home on her new wings," smiled Papai.

Tatu offered to ride back on Jasmina so Joa could take his place in the boat, and thus not spoil her fine outfit.

But Sr. Diogo said Joa's weight wouldn't make any difference in the canoe. To trust him. He was always very careful.

And sure enough, when they were all settled, the water

didn't come any higher up the boat's side than it had before. But it was very hard for Joa to keep awake and sit up straight. She was so tired. Gradually she leaned more and more against Mamai, and went fast asleep.

When the canoe ran its nose into their own soft sands, Papai lifted her and carried her to the veranda, while Tatu used the flashlight to make a path. Boy and Perla woke up to see what was going on.

"I've brought you an angel bird," Papai told them. "She fell out of the sky. And tomorrow, Perla, you can straighten out her feathers."

Boy and Perla chortled as if they thoroughly understood the joke.

VIII

Tarzan Joins the Family

"WHAT WAS THAT?" Mamai whispered. It was early morning and the Amarals were still lying in their hammocks.

Papai woke up.

"What was that?" Mamai repeated in a low voice. She was pointing toward the ceiling. "It's an animal. There it goes again."

Papai reached for his flashlight and threw a beam against the red roof tiles. Sure enough, there was a small animal on a rafter, staring into the light. It did not know which way to turn. But it made up its mind quickly and scampered away.

"It looked like an ordinary rat," Papai whispered.

"Oh, I'm so afraid of rats!" Mamai pulled the hammock sides over her until she was completely hidden. But she kept saying how awful it was for a rat to come into this sweet, clean home, and what would she do? To think of having one run right over the children's heads! In the night, too, when there was no telling what might happen.

"Don't get so excited," said Papai. "The children are perfectly safe."

"I know I'll never sleep a wink so long as that thing is in

the house," Mamai's smothered voice came out from the depths of her hammock.

"Just think a minute." Papai whispered. "How could a rat climb down a straight wall to the hammock hooks? They must have something for their feet to cling to. If we were sleeping in beds it would be different. Uncover your head, Mamai. Figure it out. If you were a rat, how would you do it?"

Mamai shivered.

"How can you say such things, Papai?—'If I were a rat!'—Horrible!"

Just the same she peeked out at the three other hammocks swung across the room.

"You're quite right, Papai," she admitted. "It would take a pretty clever rat to climb into a hammock, no matter how he went at it."

"What's that about rats?" asked Joa, waking up.

"Who said rats?" Tatu laughed at her, having been awake all the time.

"Maybe you love them, Tatu, along with your bugs and spiders and things," said Mamai.

"No, I don't even like them." Tatu made a face. "But I can tell you how to get rid of them."

"How?" asked Joa.

"Get a cat," he said.

"You mean there is no cat in all your big menagerie out in the quintal?" Papai sounded very surprised.

"No, we haven't any cat," answered Tatu.

"Are you sure you looked in all the cages and pens and tree tops, Son?"

"I'm sure."

"I am, too," Joa chimed in.

"There, Mamai. You've got a rat because you haven't got a cat. Tatu will solve your problems. And I'm sure Maria, who seems to know everything, can find you the rat catcher. And how about her finding us some coffee about now?"

Maria seemed as shocked about the rat as Mamai. She said it was probably not a house rat, though, but a wild one from the woods. Maybe it had paid them a visit to satisfy its curiosity about the new family from the south. More likely it had come for the corn on the back porch. Anyway, it would have to be got rid of.

"A cat could catch it," Tatu was ready with his idea.

"We'll get something better than a cat," smiled Maria. And she went out with the empty coffee cups.

"What do you suppose she's going to get?" asked Joa.

"A trap," Papai laughed.

"Maybe it will be a ferret," said Tatu, hopefully. "I never saw a ferret. But there is a picture of one in my zoology book at home. They are long and slim, and go everywhere a rat can. They slide in and out. And whenever Mr. Rat isn't watching, they pounce on him."

"Suppose you two lazybones ferret yourselves out of your hammocks this minute, or I'll be shaved and dressed before you are." Papai turned away from the mirror, and, quick as a flash, he lathered both their noses with his shaving brush.

"Now look at them, Mamai! What strange children we have!"

Joa sneezed because she sniffed some of the lather up her nose.

"And what funny noises they make," added Mamai, who was laughing by this time.

Of course Tatu and Joa had to get up then, to wipe the soap off their faces.

"Last one into the river is a howling monkey!" Papai dared them. And he shot out the door in his bathing trunks. They could see him running across the sand and splashing into the small waves.

For once Joa beat her brother, because Tatu couldn't find his trunks. He hunted and hunted, with Mamai helping him. He had entirely forgotten that he had hung them up to dry at the other end of the quintal. So finally he had to wear a pair of shorts.

"Ha, ha! Who's the howling monkey?" shouted Joa, when Tatu appeared at last.

They had a long swim and a big romp on the beach. And when they came in Maria had something to show them. She explained that Sr. Diogo had borrowed it from a storekeeper in the town. It was in a box on the back porch.

"What did I tell you? It's a ferret," Tatu whispered to Joa and Papai, as they followed Maria through the kitchen.

There was quite a bit of excitement on the back porch. Perla was calling shrilly to the parakeets to keep close to her. Boy was coming as fast as he could to see what Perla was fussing about. Guapo, the gray monkey, was pulling at his leash giving his warning cry of "Chico! Chico!" for all the animals to hide. And the wild birds were running to a far corner of the quintal.

Papai, Joa and Tatu peered through the slats of a wooden box to see the creature curled up inside. It raised its smooth gray head. Out shot a forked tongue! Joa ran away. But Tatu stayed, fascinated. And Papai called Mamai.

"Here's your rat catcher, Mamai," he said, as she walked through the back door.

"Yes?" Mamai came slowly and leaned over the box, not knowing just what she would see. "Oh! It's a snake! How awful!"

She drew back and covered her eyes with her hand. Then she looked again, fascinated like Tatu.

Maria stood smiling, quite proud that she was going to get rid of the rat so quickly.

"He is a very fine ratter, Senhora," she said. "We'll let him out this evening."

"You mean that snake is going to run loose around my house?" Mamai exclaimed.

"Surely, Senhora. He is very tame and harmless and he wouldn't hurt a soul. He is most intelligent, too. When he catches the rat, he will come back into his box to sleep. That's true, Senhora." Maria talked as if the snake were a real friend of hers.

Tatu had always heard about people keeping big pet snakes here in the north. And he wanted to see the snake go hunting. He wondered if it could smell his alligator tooth charm. He had left it on the museum table in the living room. And he was thinking of having José keep the tooth for him, away from the house while the snake was here. Of course charms were just a superstition. He might as well leave it there. Nothing would happen. That was what he was thinking, watching the snake's tongue shooting in and out.

"Maria!" Mamai's voice was quite stern. "You have Sr.

Diogo take that reptile right out of here. I'd rather have a million rats than that beast."

Maria said, "All right," but she looked quite hurt and disappointed. She was not so disappointed as Tatu, though. He begged his mother to try the snake just this once. Anyway, not to send it away until he could watch it awhile. If she would only look at it, she would see what a pretty pattern it had on its back.

"Manoel Octavio da Silva Amaral!" Mamai only called Tatu his real name when she was very cross. "If you would rather have that reptile here than your mother, you keep it. And I'll stay at José's house until it goes."

Of course Mamai did not really mean that, but she looked so troubled that Tatu said, "Let Sr. Diogo take it then. I don't care."

Just then, in came Sr. Diogo himself to see what was happening. The snake would go right back, he said. And he was sorry it had frightened Joa and bothered Sra. Amaral. Any time Tatu wanted to get better acquainted with it, though, the storekeeper would be glad to have him visit the store.

"And now, Mr. Snake, come along, we'll exchange you for a trap," said Sr. Diogo, as he picked up the box and smiled at all of them.

Joa came out of hiding, and Sr. Diogo gave her a special smile.

Papai looked at his watch.

"I've a good idea to take a holiday," he said. "In fact, that was what I was thinking of doing all along. How would you children like to ride out into the country with me?"

Their eyes were shining, for Papai was always finding

something exciting to do when he was not too busy.

"Would you like to go along, Mamai?" Papai asked.

"What would I ride?"

"You can have Jasmina," Joa offered generously.

"Yes, Joa can ride with me on Branquissimo," said Tatu.

"And I'll get a horse in town," said Papai.

"No, thank you. I think I'll stay right here on the cool veranda and do some tatting. I'll be very happy now that Mr. Snake is gone. But first I'll make you all some sandwiches."

When they started out, Papai and Tatu were on Branquissimo, who did not mind carrying double. And Joa was on her Jasmina. The sandwiches were wrapped up in their bundle of string hammocks and tied to her saddle.

Mamai waved good-by from the veranda as the horses walked away through the soft sand. As usual a fisherman was throwing his great net that flew out like a round of lace. The net landed at the edge of the river and sank out of sight. Then all they could see were circles on the water that grew wider and wider until they were gone. When the net was pulled in, it looked like a big wet string bag. But there were always fish in it.

"Any sting rays?" Tatu called out. He was still hoping to see a live sting ray.

The fisherman shook his head. "Not yet." That was what he always answered.

Next they came to the cotton gin, a big factory where machinery was whirring. It was North American cotton machinery that had cost a great deal of money. The city of Santarem owned it. And all the farmers brought their crop here. Cotton lay on the floor in a great snow pile, full of brown seeds. After it came out of the machine, the seeds were all gone and the fluffy cotton was packed tight in bales ready to be shipped.

Sr. Diogo always bought some of the seeds to feed the cows, who love cottonseed mixed with salt, for dessert.

On the other side of the road was a mill where rice was hulled. And near that mill was the house of Mr. Riker, a North American living in Santarem.

Mr. Riker was out in his garden this morning, tending his roses. His house was very pretty with hibiscus and bougainvillea trained between the front windows. On the front of the house was painted an American eagle.

"Good morning," Mr. Riker called out in English. "What a beautiful day!"

"Good morning," Papai called back, for he could speak English, too. "Your roses are lovely."

But Tatu and Joa only said "Good morning," for they did not know much English yet.

They clattered through the clean paved streets of the town, and turned left. Ahead they could see the road rising, and soon they had gone by the plastered town houses. The road became sandy. It ran through dry meadows, and hills appeared beyond that became almost mountains in the distance. Here and there were dark green patches, as if the jungle had splashed up out of the river, when the sandy land was made.

Tatu said the green splashes looked like islands. And Papai said that was clever of Tatu, because they were called ilhas de moto, which means "islands of forest."

"In fact," Papai went on, "we are, this minute, in the middle of a very interesting geography lesson that I have only learned myself since I came to Santarem. Let's stop and look at it." Papai reined in Branquissimo and turned him around.

Below was Santarem, with its many pretty red roofs and pink and blue walls. At the left were the twin domes of the cathedral, and the green trees of the praça. And at the right, the wharf with all sorts of boats dotted around it.

But what was most interesting, Papai pointed out that the rivers were as plain as a map from up here. The Tapajoz came flowing more than a thousand miles from the south, all green water. The other shore seemed very near. But the Tapajoz was really two miles wide, from the sandy beaches on this side to the green jungles on the other.

Beyond that point of jungle, lay the Amazon like a great yellow lake. They could scarcely see across it. From this distance it looked quiet enough, but it was moving swiftly eastward, as they well knew, five hundred miles down to the sea. And below the angle of jungle, where the two rivers came together, the green water and the yellow were fighting, until the Amazon gobbled up the great Tapajoz. For the Amazon is the mightiest river in the world.

Across the great Amazon, called the Father of All Waters, was nothing but jungle for a long distance.

"I'd love to go over there," said Tatu.

"You wouldn't get far," answered Papai. "After you pass the little farms along the shore, there is nothing. Just low rich jungle. Then there are lakes and some higher land away beyond. But no road or paths to them. And only Indians live there."

"When I'm older, I'm going to be an explorer," decided Tatu.

"Let's finish this exploration first," said Papai, turning

Branquissimo's head toward the hills and starting off again. "See what we have here. Dry sand, sandstone, and those bare rock mountains in the distance that have no trees on them at all. That is what surprised me, the dryness and lack of vegetation, for I had always thought this part of the world was steamy and wet. Now you know your Santarem geography lesson—at least enough for today."

Papai thought the children were tired of hearing so much about this. But Tatu was ready with a question.

"How did it get that way?" he asked.

"Well, ages ago, before there were any men on earth, this was all part of the great ocean. Then gradually the tips of those mountains appeared above the waters. The reason we know this, definitely, is that fossils of sea shells can be found up there. That proves it was once the bottom of the sea before it started to be the South American Continent. And that's the end of the geography lesson," smiled Papai.

"Oh, I wish I could get some of those fossil shells for my museum!" sighed Tatu. "Can't we go hunt for them today?"

"The mountains are farther away than they look. It must be fifteen miles to the Serra de Muruarú," Papai pointed to a mountain which looked as if the top had been sliced off. "It would be a good place to hunt, nice and flat after we got there. But there's no road and it would be too long a ride for you children, there and back."

Tatu looked so disappointed that Papai said he would try to buy him a fossil or two in the town, where surely someone collected them.

There were small clearings along the way, little farms of fruit trees with palm-leaf houses. Children were playing in the yards. When the Amarals called out "Bom dia!" they answered "Bom dia!" And now came a big truck lumbering along toward them. The horses quickly got out of its way on one side of the road, which was not wide enough for them and the truck, too.

Jasmina snorted. She didn't like trucks. But the truck snorted back at her, and steam poured out of its radiator cap. It was loaded with great balls of crude black rubber, freshly milked from the rubber trees. These balls weighed as much as Joa. And they bounced around against each other as the truck bumped over the sandy ruts. The driver said, "Bom dia," too, and he looked so hot that the Amarals suddenly felt warm themselves. The cool Santarem wind was blowing from the river, but the sun was burning through their hats.

The road went downhill after that, before climbing to the mountains far away. And Papai now took a little side trail that led to an ilha de moto where it looked cool and shady. Soon the trail entered the "island," and the sun was hidden by a roof of trees and vines swinging high in the air. A little opening brought them to a babbling brook, which was a perfect place to rest.

"Are you hungry?" asked Papai. "This is a fine spot to have lunch."

Of course they were. And tired as well. Besides, Jasmina and Branquissimo wanted their saddles off to cool their hot backs. And they were longing for a drink out of the brook, and for a nibble of the sweet grasses and ferns that grew along the stream. So Papai unsaddled and watered them, while Joa and Tatu unpacked the lunch.

Tatu cut several wild banana leaves. Joa laid them down for a tablecloth and set out the sandwiches. There were little tarts, some meat pies, hard boiled eggs, and fruit, besides. Mamai had fixed a fine lunch. And it looked very tempting spread out on the green tablecloth. Papai started a little fire, for now they found their camping place cool. He boiled water in a tin cup and made maté. Mamai had thought of everything, even the sugar for the tea and the salt for the eggs.

But the most thoughtful thing she had done was to wrap the lunch in those string hammocks. Papai strung these up after lunch for the siesta. It was beautiful swinging under orchids and vines, listening to the birds and wood crickets.

Many interesting things were happening in the little clearing. Tatu could not go to sleep, listening to the fruits falling into the stream. Every time, he thought it must be an animal which went *plop* into the water. And then he would see only a nut pod or a palm fruit, floating away.

While he was watching, two big lizards chased each other over the dead leaves. They ran right under his hammock down to the water. One plunged in, the other followed, and they swam and played together. Tatu had watched lizards all his life, but never before had he seen any that liked the water or could swim.

And now there was a creature moving up in a tree. It was gray, the color of the tree trunk. And it was very slow. By and by, it let itself down into a lower limb, and Tatu could really see it. A sloth! He was very much excited. No other creature could act so lazy and slothful as that. It was eating the leaves of the tree, too, just as sloths were said to do. Its claws were like hooks fastened around a branch. When it had chewed

Tatu laid the baby wildcat in his mother's lap

up all the leaves near by, it stood on its hind legs and looked around for more. The hairy forelegs went out, feeling for another branch. When the heavy front claws were safely around it, the hind legs moved up and took hold.

Tatu spoke to Joa. He didn't want her to miss this curious sight. But she was sound asleep.

The sloth heard him, though. It turned toward him, and Tatu thought the long hair on its face made it look like an old man with a thick gray beard. Then it slid slowly along the branch out of sight. Tatu was sure it was looking at him through the leaf screen. He kept his eyes on the spot until finally they closed.

There was another noise when the Amarals woke up. It sounded like a house cat being stepped on, not far away up the stream. Tatu bounded out of his hammock. He tried to walk silently over the moist, springy ground. Papai was right after him, for Tatu was always too venturesome for safety. And Joa followed in Papai's footsteps as fast as she could. In the next little clearing they all stopped short. There, stretched out full length, was a big wildcat with leopard spots. Beside it was its baby, the prettiest little thing, spotted like the mother.

"Wait here," Papai said to the children. "I think the big cat is dead, but we'll make sure she isn't just playing 'possum." Papai had his large sheath knife in his hand, for mother wildcats are dangerous. But the animal never stirred, so Papai bent down and turned it over.

"Some hunter shot at it and then lost it," said Papai. "For he surely would have wanted this beautiful skin."

The baby wildcat started to run into the bushes. It was too

young to go fast and Tatu easily caught it. At first it tried to scratch and bite him with its tiny teeth and claws. And it meowed in a wild hoarse voice, making the sound they had heard at first. Of course it was frightened. But when Tatu sat down on the ground so they could better examine the little orphan, it crept under his coat and cuddled there.

"Tarzan's hungry," said Joa. "I wish we had some milk."

"Tarzan's probably starving— Is that what you are going to call him?" asked Papai.

"I think that's a good name for him, the way he scratched me," said Tatu, examining his fingers. "It goes with his fierce voice, too."

"Now, Joa, if you hadn't eaten every last bit of lunch, you might offer some to our new friend." Papai was always teasing Joa about her big appetite.

"I didn't," protested Joa. "There's an egg left."

The yolk of a hard-cooked egg was just what Tarzan was crying for. After he had gobbled it he wanted more and acted quite tame. He rode all the way back under Tatu's buttoned coat. And when they got home Tatu laid the kitten in his mother's lap.

"Mamai, here's the cat you need to catch the rat."

"What an adorable kitten—but I've already bought the trap," she said.

IX

A Jaboti Is a Wise Creature

"WHAT KIND of meat is this?" Tatu asked. "It's awfully good."

"Capivara," answered Maria, coming out from the kitchen with another platter.

"Oh—!" Joa nearly choked.

And Tatu held his fork stock-still in the air. On it was a piece of very dark meat. It looked like mutton, but had a strong wild taste. Slowly he laid the fork down.

Mamai and Papai went on talking without paying any attention to Tatu. Presently he asked to be excused a minute, pushed back his chair and went out through the kitchen. Joa watched him and sat still without eating.

Pretty soon he came back. He looked at his sister, and said, "Sim, êle esta," which in Portuguese means, "Yes, he is there."

"What are you two talking about?" asked Mamai. "Where did you go, just now, Tatu?"

"I went out to Cap's pen to see if he were still there," Tatu replied, picking up his fork again.

"Oh, that wasn't Cap!" Maria laughed. "He's fat enough

to eat, but I bought this meat in the market today. Some hunters came across the river with a whole canoe full of it."

Joa was not sure whether she wanted to eat capivara meat or not. So she dawdled over her plate until Maria brought her a little dish of scrambled eggs. But Papai and Mamai said it was delicious, something like venison. And Tatu did not care what he ate so long as it wasn't one of his pets.

After dinner Tatu went with José from pen to pen feeding the animals, as they did every evening. And he stopped for a long visit with Cap who rubbed his prickly sides against Tatu's legs, nearly pushing him over. Then Tatu let him out for a wonderful bath in the wash tank, and promised that no one would ever use him for meat. Cap seemed grateful, and waddled back to his pen on his funny guinea pig legs, to eat more corn and grow fatter.

The pen of the jabotis seemed to be empty, and Tatu had a horrible thought that maybe they had already gone into jaboti stew without his knowing it. But José said the wise little rascals were hiding. They had probably heard the talk about Cap. Anyway they knew it was holiday time, and their lives were in danger; for everyone considers them a special delicacy.

They were in hiding, sure enough. They had covered themselves with a small pile of dry grass. And one had even dug himself a cave under the watering pan. When José dragged them out for their dinners they pretended to be dead, with their tails, heads and feet drawn inside their shells.

"You watch them," said José, "while I get some greens."

In a minute José had cut a big handful of collards and another of lettuce from the garden on stilts. And he and Tatu were laying fresh leaves in front of each jaboti's mouth, when Joa appeared with Tomás and Sara. The turtles' heads came out so slowly that no one could see them move. When they were sure it was safe, they began to nibble very quietly, ready to play dead again any moment.

"Poor little things!" exclaimed Joa. "Don't be afraid of us! We hate jaboti stew and we won't ever let Maria or Alzira get you."

Whereupon the jabotis began to chew quite noisily, and rattle around the pen, as if they were dancing with joy because they understood what she had said.

The five children finished feeding the pets, while Tarzan played around their feet. He ran from one to the other, taking bites at their ankles like a puppy.

Then they all sat down near the jabotis, on a bench made out of half a log. Tarzan was going to sleep on Joa's lap. He was licking her finger so hard with his rough tongue that she was sure the skin was coming off. The evening was lovely and cool. The orchard was sweet with orange and lemon blossoms. And the sun was beginning to go down. It was a perfect hour for story telling. So presently José asked,

"Would you like to hear the story of the 'Jaboti and the Deer'?—My grandfather told it to me."

Of course they would. Tales about the jaboti have always been favorites in Santarem. No one knows how old they are. The Indians began telling them at the time when animals and human beings could talk together. This little tortoise lives on land, where men could get well acquainted with him. He is very pretty with a high shell marked off into bright yellow and brown squares, and brown legs with vermilion polka dots on them. But most important of all, he is the wisest of all animals in the Santarem forests.

Tatu had always believed that the armadillo was the wisest animal of all. Joa had begun calling him a *tatu,* or armadillo, when she was little. So he was especially interested in hearing about the doings of these turtles, which were evidently quite as clever, from the way the tame jabotis had acted just now.

"Well," began José. "First of all the jaboti is the animal of seven talents. The Indians discovered that a long time ago when they began to call him jaboti. Let's each of us name a talent. First of all, I say that the jaboti can outwit men, who think they are the smartest creatures on earth. What next?"

"He can go to the sky and attend the festivals there," said Sara. "No one ever found out how he gets there, but he is always the first guest to arrive."

"I guess he can act as crazy as a monkey when he wants to," said Joa, who had watched them.

"No river is too wide for him to cross, yet he's a land animal and never learned to swim," said José.

"The jaboti can win a fight with the tapir, and everybody knows the tapir is the biggest and strongest beast of the jungle," said Sara.

After this there was a silence.

"That makes five things," said José. "What are the other two, anyway?"

"He makes bad children good," said Tomás. "I remember when I was little and wouldn't obey, they put a teeny-weeny jaboti in the bath with me. It was supposed to tame me. I was always good right away, but I think it was because the little turtle was so pretty and interesting that I forgot to be bad any longer."

Now it was Tatu's turn, since he was the only one who hadn't spoken. How could he be expected to know about the talents of the jaboti? He thought fast. And suddenly he said,

"The jaboti can run faster than the deer. Isn't that what your story is going to be about, José?"

"How did you know, Tatu?"

"Because the jaboti can do everything, can't he?" answered Tatu.

That made the seventh talent. And José began his story about the "Jaboti and the Deer."

"Before there were any men on earth, the animals had the plains and the forests to themselves. They could do anything they wanted anywhere they wished, for there were no blowguns and poisoned darts, nor bows and arrows to kill them. They had only to watch out for each other. That was not so hard, since every creature was given a special gift from heaven by which he could take care of himself.

"The deer, for instance, was very beautiful. All the other animals admired him because of his soft pretty skin and his graceful dancing legs. His horns were not much good for fighting jaguars and pumas, but he could run a lot faster than they could and so get away from their hungry jaws.

"The jaboti was able to protect himself by going into his hard shell when danger came. He could tuck in his legs, arms, tail and head. Then he had to use his wits, for he was too small and insignificant to get by any other way. And, of course, he was about the slowest runner in the forest.

"One day the deer met the jaboti on the jungle path.

" 'Where are you going, jaboti?' asked the deer.

" 'I am going to the Crystal Lake, about three days' journey, to get assaí fruit. I hear there are fine trees of it there and the fruit is now ripe.'

" 'Three days' journey to Crystal Lake!' the deer laughed aloud. 'Why I was there just a couple of hours ago. But of course I'm not a clumsy little thing like you with my feet stuck close to my body. I leap along across the campo as fast as a bird flies.'

"To prove it, the deer took a few flying leaps down the path and back. The jaboti had to pretend that was wonderful. But inside he was, as always, very angry at being looked down upon. So he put his wits to work.

" 'You are surely a fine runner,' he said to the deer. 'But I can go faster than you think. I'll bet I can beat you in a race.'

" 'What will you bet?'

" 'I'll bet you my shell to make soup in, against a big branch of assaí fruit you will bring me from Crystal Lake.'

"Now the deer did not know that he couldn't make soup in a jaboti's shell, for water can be put over the very hottest fire in one of their shells and it never will boil. I tried it once," said José, "and it's true. A lot of steam comes off, but the water never bubbles."

Then José went on with his story. "Suspecting nothing, the deer leaped away toward Crystal Lake to get the biggest branch of assaí fruit he could find to keep his end of the bargain.

" 'Don't hurry,' the jaboti called after him. 'I'm so tired after my long walk I couldn't run today, anyway. But I'll be ready first thing in the morning.'

"Meanwhile the jaboti sent out a call to all his family living everywhere, in the jungle. You could hear their little polka-dotted legs rattling everywhere along the low jaboti paths to their secret meeting place.

"When they were all together, the jaboti said, 'Brothers, I am in a dangerous situation. I have challenged the deer to a race and if I lose he is to get my shell, so I will die.'

"They all began to talk at once—what a foolish thing!— why, the deer was the fastest runner in the world! The jaboti bade them be quiet. He had a plan.

"He was afraid to tell the plan out loud, for those busybodies, the monkeys, are always sneaking around in the branches above, listening for gossip they can repeat. So he crept from relative to relative and whispered in each one's ear. It was a pretty smart plan, though not at all honorable. However, all the relatives approved, and the meeting broke up.

"The next morning the deer came prancing down the forest path with a beautiful plume of assaí fruit nodding between his horns.

" 'Jaboti, here is the fruit. Are you ready?' he asked.

" 'Yes, I am ready,' answered the jaboti.

" 'Then come on.' Whereupon the deer turned back down the path toward the open prairie. He was laughing because the jaboti did not follow. The poor thing was too slow to get started.

" 'Oh, I can't run out there,' exclaimed the jaboti. 'I am a forest dweller and not used to the plains. Now you live in both the woods and the fields, so it is just the same to you.

And besides you have more advantages, with your long legs and practice in running. So it is fair that you give in to me in this.'

"That did seem fair enough to the deer, who could win wherever he ran. He said, 'All right. It shall be as you wish.'

" 'Then let's start. One—two—three— Go! shouted the jaboti, shooting off through the underbrush as fast as he could.

"The deer took his time, chuckling as he went and slinging a few insults behind him. But suddenly the jaboti answered from the path beyond.

"The deer started to run after that, when he had just been walking before.

" 'Where are you now, jaboti?' he asked pretty soon.

" 'Here,' the jaboti answered from up front somewhere, and the deer hurried faster.

" 'Now where are you?' called the deer, running as fast as he could down the rough crooked path.

" 'I'm winning!' called the jaboti, still ahead.

"At that the deer increased his speed until he could hardly breathe.

" 'Hurry if you want to catch up with me,' the jaboti sang out, away ahead by this time.

"The deer had no breath left to reply. But he went so crazy at being beaten that he did not watch where he was going and ran smash into a tree!

"This proud and beautiful creature was dead.

"Then from all along the route came the little jabotis, their short polka-dot legs twinkling through the bushes. For all the relatives had run this race. They had stationed themselves under the bushes along the path at regular places. So every time the deer had heard a call, it was a different jaboti just in front of him. That was the smart plan they had agreed to, at the council meeting. And now the jaboti had won over the deer. That would be something to tell at the next festival in the sky.

"They all gathered together around the branch of assaí fruit the deer had brought from Crystal Lake, and had a great celebration eating the fruit and boasting about their wonderful scheming that they thought made them superior to all the other animals. And that's the end of this story, but there are a whole lot more about the jaboti." José's audience clapped as he finished.

"I know a fable about 'The Tortoise and the Hare' that is something like that," said Tatu. "I read it in my book of *Aesop's Fables.*"

"Go on. Tell it," said Sara.

"I'll make it very short," said Tatu.

"Once the tortoise challenged the hare to a race, and the hare laughed just as your deer did, José. But the hare accepted. He was sure to win because he could go as far in one hop as the tortoise in many steps. They started even. The tortoise ran as fast as his short legs would carry him. But the hare stopped to eat and play. He thought he could easily catch up any time he wanted to. Before he knew it the tortoise got far ahead. The hare ran and ran and ran as fast as he could to make up for lost time. But in spite of the long hops he made, the tortoise got there first. He won by small patient steps, one after the other, and that's the moral of the fable."

"I can tell a story about our parrot," said Sara. "It's short, too. Our parrot's name is Beleza, because she is so pretty, with a green body and red on her head and under her wings. She is a great pet, and follows my mother around the house like a puppy. In fact, Mamai has to fasten her up on her perch sometimes when the whole family is home so she won't get trampled on. When she thinks she is going to be tied up, she hides.

" 'Beleza, Beleza,' Mamai calls. 'Where are you?'

" 'Dona Maria, here I am,' she answers from under the bed. But by the time my mother gets there the parrot is behind a chair. 'Dona Maria, here I am,' she says, and runs to a new place. That is her way of playing hide-and-seek.

"We live farther down the river, and every year when the water rises we have to move to high ground. That is a big job, for we take all the stock, the cows, calves, pigs, goats and everything we need for farming. We have two houses and two farms, one for the dry season and another when the rains come."

All nodded in agreement, for that is the custom on the Amazon. In most places the river rises forty feet during the rainy season, and covers everything for miles and miles.

"Well," Sara went on with her story, "the river came up very fast last year. We had to hurry with the moving. Everybody was so busy that Beleza was left behind. Afterward, my mother remembered hearing her say, 'Dona Maria, here I am,' then she forgot about it. Beleza hid a little too long that time. When Mamai missed her, it was too late. The waters had covered our river farm and we couldn't go back. We just gave Beleza up for lost.

"When the rains stopped and the river went down again,

we moved back, as usual. The first time my mother walked out the forest path, there was a great flutter in the trees.

" 'Dona Maria, here I am!' dozens of parrots yelled out at once.

"Beleza had taught the whole flock to say that. They were so proud of themselves they kept yelling enough to deafen my mother. And there was Beleza, herself! She flew down from a high tree to a low bush beside the path and hopped on my mother's shoulder.

" 'Dona Maria, here I am,' she said.

"There she was, as saucy and tame as ever! And she was so glad to see my mother that she cooed and shook her feathers and rubbed her head against my mother's ears all the way back to the house. I guess this year she won't let herself be left behind again."

The children were quiet at the end of the story. It was nearly dark, and they were wondering what they would do next. Then suddenly there was a snort behind them. The log bench tipped over, and they were all sprawling on the ground. It was a low bench, so no one was hurt, but everyone was taken by surprise.

When they picked themselves up, there stood Peixe-Boi, at a safe distance, laughing at them. He had opened the gate of the quintal again and sneaked up behind them to play this trick. He was so much pleased at the way it came out that he walked over to the raised garden and began helping himself to the vegetables.

José ran to the fence yelling for his grandfather to come quickly or the garden would be destroyed. The rest of the children were trying to drive the bull away, but he just shook his horns at them and went on eating.

Fortunately Sr. Diogo was having a cup of coffee with Maria and Alzira in the kitchen. He came running, and when Peixe-Boi saw him, he trotted away. He went out the gate he had opened and did not stop until he was in his solitary confinement pen. There he waited for Sr. Diogo to put up the bars. For he knew he had been a very bad bull, and he might as well take his punishment. Anyway, he would be able to get out as soon as everyone was asleep.

But Sr. Diogo was wise to him this time, and tied every bar with a sailor's knot he had learned when he was in the Brazilian navy. Even a smart bull like Peixe-Boi could never figure out how to untie it.

X

Papai Has a Secret

JOA AND TATU wanted to do some shopping in Santarem the day before New Year's. Tatu wanted fireworks, rockets and crackers to make a noise at midnight. Joa needed colored crepe paper to cut out streamers and other decorations for trimming the house in celebration.

When they trotted into town on Jasmina and Branquissimo, they were certainly surprised to see all the wares of the stores dumped right on the sidewalks, plus all the household furniture of every house in town. Joa and Tatu were surely the strangers in town, for did they not know that no merchant could find anything for his customers on the annual cleaning day before the New Year?

"Crepe paper!" the clerk struck his forehead. "Where did we put the crepe paper?"

Finally the paper was found under a heap of tobacco, which, of course, gave it a strong scent. Joa sniffed it, and the clerk said such a perfume was worth paying extra for.

They walked on through the middle of the street. There was no room on the sidewalks, of course. Such activity of sweeping and scrubbing and scouring. Above the din in the houses they could hear everyone singing and whistling. The air was full of a strong odor of soapsuds so that you could even smell what was going on. When they finally made their way to the shop of the fireworks maker, he shook his head and said that he had been too busy finishing his orders. Now he would have to do his cleaning in the middle of the night. With much good-natured grumbling, however, he finally sold Tatu the rockets and firecrackers. As they left, Tatu said that it looked as though everyone in Santarem was moving at once with all their furniture on the sidewalks waiting for the moving van.

When they got home, their own things were out on the front veranda—that is, all but the museum. The tile floors were still wet. And Mamai said Joa and Tatu would have to dust their exhibits as soon as things dried off a bit.

By the time midnight came, everything was in order again. Even the roadways and pavements had been washed clean. The rockets and fireworks, the cathedral bells, the siren of the electric light works, and whistles on ships and launches, all went off at the same moment. And the New Year started in a spotless town.

Everyone went to sleep feeling proud and happy, to dream of the good things they would have to eat tomorrow.

Then in a week came the Day of the Kings, with gifts for all children. Tatu was surprised with a whole set of sea shells and fish fossils from the top of the mountain. And, best of all her presents, Joa liked a doll lace-maker. The doll was perfect, sitting before a little pillow with real lace on the pins, and the tiniest bobbins full of thread.

So the holidays had come and gone.

But Papai still had a surprise for them. He looked mysterious. He pinched Joa's cheek, gave Tatu little slaps on the back, and kept saying, "Guess what I've got on my mind?"

Mamai always smiled when he teased like this. She knew all about the surprise, of course, but she wouldn't tell.

Then came the day when Papai could not keep the secret any longer. An ox-cart rumbled along the beach from town and Peixe-Boi marched out to meet his relative. Here was an animal that had to work. It had a wooden yoke fastened to its horns which kept it from tossing its head as he did. Tied to the yoke were two chains that drew the cart.

Peixe-Boi looked at this captive member of his family that now lowered its head to pull the heavy load through the sand. The chains rattled. The cart wheels creaked. And the driver ran alongside, poking the ox with a long pole when it wanted to stop.

Peixe-Boi raised his head high. He shook his horns, snorted, and switched his tail. Then he walked away, as if he wanted everybody to know that this working animal was no brother of his.

Tatu was laughing because Peixe-Boi was acting so superior, when the cart came straight toward the veranda.

Maria heard the creaking wheels, and the driver yelling, "Whoa!" She came out on the veranda and said Sr. Amaral had left word to unload right here by the steps.

The man set down pieces of salted pirarucú fish that looked like rough boards. He lifted out baskets of mandioca meal, a sack of green coffee, another of oranges, lemons and bananas, cans of guava paste and quince marmalade, cases of bottled water and pop, and, last of all, a bag of charcoal.

Then Papai himself arrived. His secret was out. He was taking a business trip and his family was going along.

"I had to rent a launch to carry me up the Tapajoz River, and I thought I might as well get one big enough for all of us," he said.

What fun!

Joa's eyes shone with excitement. And Tatu began to get his things together right away. He straightened out his fishing lines, and asked Mamai to mend a hole in his butterfly net. He bought chloroform. Maria helped find corks for empty bottles to put specimens in, and she shined the rust off his tin bug box. She seemed pleased when he promised to bring her some new bugs she had never seen before. But she said she would appreciate it more if he and Joa would help roast the coffee for their trip.

Coffee was always roasted out in the quintal. There was a rough fireplace there, made of a few loose stones. Maria made a fire, and Tatu fanned it until nothing was left but coals. Then Maria partly filled her pan with green coffee berries. She shook it over the coals until the berries were smoking and very brown.

Maria's coffee mill was part of a log, set up on end. The center was hollowed out. She poured the hot berries into this hollow, handed Tatu a hard wooden club, and said, "Here you are."

Tatu's work was to pound the coffee with the end of the club until it was powder. When he was tired, Joa could pound for awhile.

It was quite tedious and quickly made the children's arms ache. For, by the time one lot was ground and put into a sack to be carried on the journey, Maria had another browned and ready. There must be enough to last at least a week.

Tatu would not admit he was tired. And Joa wanted to show she was as good as Tatu. But both were surely glad when it was over. By that time the whole neighborhood had smelled the delicious odor, and knew something important was happening at the Amarals'.

Early next morning the launch arrived. It anchored in deep water out in front of the house. The Brazilian flag was flying from the stern, looking very pretty. And a canoe was trailing behind at the end of a rope.

A man on board pulled the canoe up alongside and climbed into it, followed by a younger man. They paddled ashore. This was Captain Santos and his helper, Alfredo.

All the family, including Sr. Diogo and José, helped load the canoe with food, hammocks, beach and camp chairs, and suitcases. When all the baggage was aboard, the canoe came back for the passengers. And at that moment, Tarzan ran out ready to play.

"Tarzan wants to go along, Papai. Please let him," begged Joa.

"He'll always be under our feet," said Mamai. "There are runs in nearly all my best stockings already because of that wildcat."

"But Mamai, you are not going to wear your best stockings on this trip," said Joa.

"Oh, all right. Let him come then." Mamai gave in as always. "But do bring a leash so you can tie him up once in awhile."

"If Joa takes a pet, I want one, too," announced Tatu.

"I might have known it," Mamai said to herself, patiently.

Papai answered that was only fair. But Tatu would have to make up his mind pretty fast.

"All I ask," said Mamai, "is that you don't bring along one of the horses—or that huge scratchy Cap."

"Well—which will it be?" asked Papai.

"I choose Guapo," decided Tatu, already on his way to the back porch. "No one ever pays much attention to him. He never has a really good time."

Tatu was back in a moment with the gray monkey in his arms. All this had made quite a delay and Captain Santos was looking impatient. But at last everybody was aboard, including the two animals. Alfredo tied the canoe trailer by its rope. Captain Santos started the motor and they chugged away, waving to Alzira, Maria, Sr. Diogo and José, back on the beach.

Mamai went to work at once making a home out of the launch. Papai told her she was very good at this. And Mamai answered that she had had plenty of practice, and was getting more every day.

She untied bundles and took out four prettily painted gourds to use for drinking cups; four pottery dishes that would do for both soup bowls and plates; and a big red casserole which she filled with fruit.

Then she unrolled some braided palm-leaf mats. The big ones were for the floor of the deck, the little ones for the table. Suitcases went into the cabin, which was so tiny that the family could only stay in it by sitting on each other's laps. It would be fine and dry if there was a storm, though. The rainy season was due any time. But Mamai said meanwhile

it came in very handy for shutting up Tarzan with the suitcases, so she could finish her work in peace.

Then Papai strung up the hammocks on deck, and opened
out the striped canvas deck chairs and camp stools.

The hammocks started swinging in every direction with
the motion of the launch. Joa's lace boys and girls were dancing in the breeze. Tatu's "coat of many colors" was dazzling.
Mamai's white lacy bed was rocking invitingly. And Tatu
said Papai's rainbow hammock surely had a bag of gold
hidden under it.

In a few minutes their home on the launch looked very
gay. And everybody was happy, except Guapo, who had
never traveled before. He crept under the table and stayed
there, frightened at the noise of the motor.

"Oh, I do hope Guapo's not going to be seasick!" said Tatu.

Papai laughed. "Can you imagine monkeys being seasick,
when they're born in treetops that sway much more than
boats?" he asked.

Papai seated Mamai in her deck chair, and then settled
himself in another. The children sat down, Tatu still watching Guapo.

"Solid comfort!" said Papai, stretching his legs.

"But where is the kitchen?" asked Joa.

"You don't mean you're hungry already, when we're
scarcely started?" smiled Papai.

"Not yet," answered Joa. "I was only wondering how we're
going to get lunch."

"We have to wait for Tatu to catch a fish," Papai's eyes
were twinkling.

"Do we?" Joa took Papai seriously. "Why, he hasn't even

started fishing yet."

"I'll catch you a fish, Joa," boasted Tatu. "Watch and see."

Tatu opened the door of the cabin to get his tackle box. And out ran Tarzan, dashing between Tatu's legs. He had outwitted a boy, and that made him feel very frisky.

Mamai put her feet up on the rungs of a camp chair while Joa caught the wildcat and tried to make him lie quietly on her lap.

Tatu came back from the cabin with his fishing box, and chose a line and hooks. He rigged them together, using three hooks. And then he found the right kind of banana in Mamai's casserole. Only a certain kind would do, one that was a deep yellow inside. And it had to be just ripe enough, but not too ripe. He peeled it, cut it into little cubes, and fixed a cube firmly on each hook.

Then he let out yards and yards of line, until the bait was trailing far behind them. There was a strong current which was trying to push the launch back to Santarem, so it was moving slowly, and Tatu could see the little ripple of his bait on top of the water.

Captain Santos came to see how they were getting along. He said everything was going nicely now, so he could leave Alfredo at the steering wheel for awhile. He looked at Tatu's fishing line, and then at Papai. And both men smiled. They didn't think Tatu could catch anything this way. But let the little boy try. That was what their looks said.

Tatu was busy tying his line to the railing and did not notice. But Joa understood. And now she was sure there would not be any fish for her lunch. She was pretty busy herself, too, keeping Tarzan amused so he would not leap down and start playing and scratching everyone's feet and ankles.

Besides, Captain Santos began pointing out places along the shore and telling about the great river. And that was so interesting that even Tatu left his line to come and listen.

They had their last view of Santarem. It was too far away to see any special house. The whole town looked as if it were floating at the edge of the water. And reaching toward them was the beautiful shining gold beach with low white waves between it and the dark water. Then they rounded a headland, and Santarem disappeared.

Meanwhile Guapo was peering at all of them from behind a table leg. At last he decided there could not be much danger with so many friends near, and slowly he crept out.

"Come, Guapo! Nice Guapo!" Tatu coaxed him.

Then Tarzan spied him and took a flying leap through the air before Joa knew what was happening. The kitten landed before the startled monkey could draw back. And the two animals crouched, staring at each other. Of course, they had already become acquainted on the back porch at home. But neither of them had thought of being friends, for grown-up wildcats are enemies of monkeys. And Tarzan would be grown up some day. But at this age he was more of a kitten than a wildcat. At any rate, he wanted to play and he wanted Guapo to like him. So he rolled over like any pet kitty. And he looked so sweet and harmless that Guapo put out a little hand and touched Tarzan's fuzzy tan stomach. When his hand was not scratched or bitten, he came closer. Tarzan began boxing at him with both front paws, very gently at first. In no time at all, they were romping together like two puppies, then playing hide-and-seek like kittens. It was very amusing, and the Amarals forgot to watch where the launch was going.

Just around the next point of land, the river was suddenly growing very wide. They were coming into what looked like a lake. The wind was blowing stronger and white caps were springing up everywhere. Captain Santos said he would have to go now, for Alfredo would need him to steer through this part of the river. It was ten miles wide, and very tricky.

He said they must watch for a beautiful little bay with a lonely flat-topped mountain guarding it. The small mountain was called Altar de Chão or Earth Altar, because of its shape. And the little harbor and town had the same name. These mountains are very peculiar, and do not exist anywhere else in the world, he told them, getting up from his chair.

"Oh, look, Tatu! Your line!" shouted Joa.

Everybody rushed to the railing, and away out in the river, leaping in the air and trying to get away, was a fish. Tatu had hooked one after all.

Slowly he drew it in, a big silver beauty with black stripes. When it lay flopping on the deck at last, Papai and Captain Santos looked at each other again and smiled. But this time the smiles meant, "We were wrong, weren't we?"

"Here is your fish, Joa," Tatu said, proudly. He took the hook out of its mouth, and held it toward his sister. The fish was still wet and jumping, and Joa was a little afraid of it.

"What can I do with it?" she asked, drawing away.

"I'll take it to Alfredo, if you like," said Captain Santos. "He was just wondering what he should cook for lunch, and he will love to grill it for you over his charcoal fire."

XI

Up the Tapajoz

ON THE AFTERNOON of that first exciting day on the launch, they came to the great rubber plantations owned by Mr. Henry Ford, of Detroit. This was one of the sights Papai had come up the Tapajoz to see. The name on modern dock buildings was Belterra, which means Beautiful Land. Captain Santos explained that Belterra was the new plantation, and the trees here were not yet old enough to tap. The original plantation, farther up the river, was called Fordlandia.

The great black rubber balls lying on the wharf did not come from the Ford property, but were being shipped away, by neighbors who went after the wild trees in the forest.

Once, the Captain told them, this whole country had been rich with the money made out of wild rubber. That was in the days before automobiles, when rubber was used mostly for making raincoats, overshoes, boots, combs and such small articles. Enough of it came out of these jungles to send all over the world, and to use here in Brazil, as well.

Anyone could tap the trees growing on his own land, or in the forests that no one owned. But it was against the law to gather seeds, or to allow them to go out of Brazil. That was to keep other countries from starting to grow rubber, and taking away some of Brazil's trade.

But finally an English visitor stole some of the seeds and hid them in his trunk. He took them back to England with him, and had them planted in the botanical garden in London. They grew. And at length there were enough young plants to send out to England's tropical colonies in the Orient. In a few years, there were great rubber groves there, in the Malay States, and in Dutch Sumatra, as well as in many other places.

The trees were planted close together as in an orchard. They were not widely separated, as they were in the Brazilian jungles. Thus the rubber could be gathered quickly and easily. One man could bring in as much in a day as many men did before, when hunting it in the wilds. So it could be sold cheaper than Brazilian rubber. And soon it did not pay to tap the jungle trees any longer. The Brazilian rubber gatherers were all out of work. And the rich rubber merchants became poor. So this part of Brazil was no longer prosperous.

Captain Santos could remember the old prosperous days. There were great balls and banquets in Santarem. And people in silks and velvets were traveling on the river steamers. They wore diamonds, and big gold chains, carried gold-headed canes in their hands and gold cigar cases in their pockets. In fact they had as many things as possible made of gold and silver. Oh, it had all been very fine indeed!

Then there was a long time when the world forgot Brazilian rubber and Brazilians only gathered enough for their own overshoes and raincoats.

That was before Mr. Ford started Fordlandia. There had

been enough trouble getting it going. When they transplanted trees from the woods, the trees became sick. No one knew what to do about that at first. Then they remembered that the English and Dutch plantations in the Far East were started with Brazilian seeds. They had done famously. So expert rubber men were sent for who brought living rubber trees from the Orient. These were grafted onto the sick trees, which immediately got well and started to grow.

Things had been going fairly well ever since. But rubber trees grow very slowly, and it was a long time before the trees at Fordlandia were ready for tapping. Of course, now the world needs all the rubber it can get. Captain Santos seemed to think that the future looked a whole lot brighter for Brazilian rubber.

When the launch was tied up at the Belterra dock, an automobile appeared on the road above. It was Papai's friend, coming to show them the plantations.

The rubber trees were tall, and stood in straight rows. Men were working underneath them, keeping the ground neat and free from underbrush.

But much more interesting were the villages where the managers and workers lived. Papai said these were just like little towns in the United States, with houses built in North American style. The bungalows were made of wood, quite different from the homes in Santarem, which were built of stone, or of a mixture of stone and clay. They had wide verandas, too, screened against flies and mosquitoes. The flower gardens in front of them were very pretty, much like those in Santarem. Several even had green lawns, which was very unusual.

A little boy and girl were playing on the grass. These were North American children. But when the car stopped and Papai called out a question in English, they answered in Portuguese, for they had lived here a long time.

After a visit to the school, the store, and the hospital, Papai said he wanted to see how the new rubber trees were tapped. So a man who was especially good at this, used his little sharp rubber tapper's ax, and showed exactly how it was done. By first holding the tool slanting in one direction, and then in the other, he made a neat groove. He had to be very careful to cut only through the bark, and not to make this channel too wide, for that would hurt the tree.

Then he fastened a cup at the base of the cut for the sap to flow into. He showed them other trees whose cups were already nearly full of rubber. It was white, like thick milk. The rubber had run down the trunk of one tree and dried there in a thin film. He pulled it off, and it was a white elastic band. Then he cut a forked stick, and fastened the ends of the rubber band to it. This made a perfect slingshot, which he gave to Tatu. He reminded the boy that some Indian had done the same thing years and years ago, and thus invented the slingshot. It had proved to be such a good weapon that by the time the white man came here, the Indians could aim so well with it that they could kill a bird on the wing.

Tatu was pleased to receive the slingshot, of course, but he said he would keep it in his museum, for, with the story connected with it, it was really an Indian relic.

After they had seen everything, they were invited to an American home to supper. And it turned out to be the very house where they had seen the boy and girl playing on the lawn. Their names were John and Margaret. A separate small table was set in the dining room for the four children, so they could get acquainted. Nearly the entire supper was from North America. First there was canned tomato soup. Then there was cold baked ham that tasted of spice, and was quite different from Brazilian ham. It came out of a big tin, but it tasted quite good. Canned corn and lima beans were served with it. But the best dish was the dessert, which was real American apple pie with ice cream on top.

Tatu and Joa thought the supper quite strange. They liked it, but not so much as Mamai and Papai did, for they had eaten these unusual things many times before, at the homes of their North American friends in Rio de Janeiro.

After supper, they all drove down to the dock together. And John and Margaret came aboard to meet Tarzan and Guapo, who were already in bed. Guapo woke up only long enough to shake hands. Then he went right to sleep again. But Tarzan was ready for a romp, and raced around in his crazy way until John and Margaret had to go ashore.

The moon came out. The launch chugged up the river to a quiet little bay, where they anchored for the night. The howling monkeys on shore set up a great shrieking to warn all forest people that dangerous human beings were in the neighborhood. And along the shore somewhere, a spotted jaguar kept going, "Hough!" He made this noise between a cough and a roar to warn them that jaguars are not at all afraid of men.

But the Amarals were perfectly safe in the launch, out in the water, listening to the night sounds. It was lovely in the moonlight, with a soft breeze swinging their hammocks and blowing the mosquitoes away. And before they knew it, the sun was looking over the forest at them.

The little bay seemed very friendly with no signs of jaguars or howling monkeys anywhere. There were no houses in sight either. But several herons, long-legged egrets, and a pair of flamingoes were standing in the water, fishing for their breakfasts. The beach was clean and sandy. So all the Amarals hopped out of hammocks and into bathing suits. Then they went ashore in the canoe for a lovely swim, while the long-legged birds spread their wings and floated up into the nearest tree, where they sat patiently waiting for the noisy human visitors to go away.

Meanwhile, Alfredo was making coffee in the bow of the launch. His kitchen was a flat rock laid on the deck behind a shelter of canvas. This held a charcoal fire, and his pots. His kitchen table was a packing box. The bathers sat in camp style around the fire, using condensed milk—out of a tin—in their coffee, and eating rolls Captain Santos had bought at the bakery in Fordlandia. They had a new fruit the North Americans had planted there. It was called grapefruit, although it was nothing at all like grapes. Indeed, it was rather sour, and quite bitter. Although they put sugar on it, no one liked it. So they finished breakfast with some sweet ripe bananas.

And then away they went, keeping close to shore, and hoping that something interesting would appear soon.

They had not long to wait until they came to a charming inlet, with a creek and sandy bank on one side and a great cliff of red clay on the other. Single tall Brazil nut trees stood around a tiny house of palm leaves. And out in front of it

Guapo woke up only long enough to shake hands, but Tarzan was **ready**
for a romp

a man was working at a table.

He called out to the launch and asked if they would sell him some kerosene for his lantern. He thought they were peddlers going up the river to trade.

Captain Santos said he was not a peddler, but he could spare some kerosene.

That was too bad, the man said, for he had no money to pay. He could only exchange some of the things he was making. But maybe the Captain would not like to do that since he was not a trader.

No one should be out in the wilderness without a light at night, with all the wild creatures around, Captain Santos said, so he steered the launch into the creek. Then they all saw that the man was making beautiful big rubber balls.

Captain Santos held his launch close to the sand bank and all scrambled ashore. First the trade was made for the precious kerosene, one quart of oil for three of the balls. Tatu thought this was very little, for each one was as big as his head, and the colors were lovely. Captain Santos said the streaky blue one was for Joa, and the red and white one was for Tatu. The third, which was green and yellow, the Brazilian colors, he would keep as a present for his own little grandson back home.

Tatu was thinking about doing some trading, himself. For there were two more balls of red, white and blue, which were the United States colors, that would be lovely gifts for John and Margaret. But what did he have that a grown man, and such a clever one, would want?

The only thing Tatu had with him that he really valued was Guapo. But he could not part with the monkey for anything. Then suddenly he thought of his tackle box and how important fish hooks are to everyone along the Tapajoz.

The man was delighted to get some fish hooks, for his own stock of hooks was low and the tucanaré season was coming. He wanted to make some artificial flies out of parrot feathers, for this fish is as wily as brook trout and has very fancy tastes. He showed Tatu how to make one of these flies, tying the feathers to the hook so it looked like a small butterfly. And also how he twisted a line out of the strong fibers from pineapple leaves, which are almost invisible in the water. It was an outfit to fool any hungry fish. Tatu planned to copy it and catch some tucanaré, which are most delicious.

But he was even more interested in seeing how this fisherman made the rubber balls, especially since he was now the owner of three of them. So the man took up the work that had been interrupted when they came.

Sitting around, partly dried, were balls of various sizes modeled out of red clay from the cliff. There were jars of dyes, too, from plants that grew right here in the doorway. These materials were ready to be used with a pot of milky white rubber fresh from the rubber trees up the creek a little way.

First the man spread a thin coat of the liquid rubber over his table. Then he smeared it with dye and let it dry. Next he cut it in long strips about an inch wide. After that he picked up one of the red clay balls and rolled it over the table, across the strips. They stuck to it. He rolled and rolled until the clay was well covered. In fact, there were several layers of strips stuck on top of each other. But all the time he had been careful to leave a small hole where the red clay showed through. Now the main work was done. His heavy clay ball was all covered with colored rubber. The thing to do next was to get the clay out.

So he put the ball to soak in water, to soften the clay. Afterward, he said, he would work the clay out of the hole, a little at a time until the ball was hollow. Then he would blow air into the hole, and quickly seal it with fresh rubber. They could look at the finished balls and see how it had been done. He bounced one of them on the ground to show how hard and fine they were. It flew up into the branches of the tree, much higher than the house, and fell down to go on bouncing many times by itself. That was because the rubber was so fresh and elastic. One might say the ball was still alive, since it had been flowing through the tree that very morning.

The ball had startled a flock of gold colored butterflies, by bouncing into a damp place where they were resting and taking a drink. They flew up in a shining cloud, and Tatu could have got some fine specimens if only he had been able to get his butterfly net in time. He rushed to the cabin, but by the time he got back, the insects were away out in the river. There were so many that their shadow looked black, moving across the water.

Tatu would have plenty of time for collecting, and for fishing, too, Papai said, for he had to make several stops to see some other plantations, when the children and Mamai would have to stay on board. And this reminded Papai that they had better be going along.

So they said good-by to the maker of rubber balls, who

was sorry they could not stay longer. Tatu and Joa thought that he must be very lonely all by himself in the little palm-leaf house where he never had any visitors for weeks at a time.

XII

They Would Not Forget Itaituba

PAPAI WAS ASHORE with Captain Santos, looking at tonka bean trees back in the country, where he said it was too rough for Mamai and the children. They were waiting for him, in the launch anchored in a quiet bay, out of the river's worst current.

And at last Tatu was really fishing, using his line made out of pineapple leaf fiber, with a fly of parrot feathers that looked like one of those golden butterflies he'd missed. He could see the tucanaré sliding in and out of the shadow of the boat. But he could not get one of them to bite at his hook, although he fished just as the rubber-ball maker told him to. He would drop his fly on the top of the water, and let it float off on the current until it sank below the surface. Then when he saw a tucanaré look at it and felt the fish strike, he would pull in the line with a quick movement. But nothing ever happened. Only the school of fish shot away like flashes of lightning, and he had to wait patiently for others to come along.

Joa was fishing, too. She was throwing her line over the other side of the boat, so hers would not become tangled with her brother's. Her bait was pieces of meat. And both children were using bamboo poles that Alfredo had cut for them along the river bank.

Joa did not care much for fishing, especially when she didn't catch anything. And actually she wasn't very good at it, either. Soon she stopped watching her line, and began poking the end of her pole at Tarzan who was trying to attract her attention. He leaped up and seized it with both paws, for that was what he was hoping would happen. He kept showing his rough little tongue and needle-sharp teeth, as his wide red mouth opened and shut. Out of it came his hoarse growls and wild "meows," that sounded like a house cat being stepped on. But this only meant that Tarzan was having a good time.

"Do you mind if I tie up to your launch?" a voice spoke right beside Tatu and made him jump.

And there was the tiniest dugout canoe, with a little sun-browned woman in it. She was wearing a bright red skirt, and had a fishpole beside her.

"Of course not. You are welcome," replied Tatu politely.

"This is one of the best fishing spots in this neighborhood," she explained, throwing Tatu her rope. "Have you had any luck?"

Tatu tied the rope to the rail, and shook his head.

"There are lots of tucanaré around," he said. "But I don't know how to land them."

The little woman laughed. "If you had five hungry children to feed as I have, you would land them all right. My husband is away cutting rubber, and I have to find all the food for my family."

She did not waste a second before dropping her line into

the river. Tatu saw it was just like his, and the fly, too, was several small parrot feathers hiding the hook.

Swish! up through the air flashed a fine tucanaré right into her boat. The hook was out of its mouth and back in the river quicker than Tatu's eyes could follow it. Then, swish! and another tucanaré was jumping about in the bottom of the canoe. Again and again, the fish seemed to leap out for the little woman, almost of their own accord. Joa came to watch beside Tatu, both of them holding their breaths for fear they might spoil Mrs. Red-Skirt's luck. But there was no need of that. She kept on picking the fish out of the water until she had twelve, two apiece for her and her children, enough for both lunch and supper.

And then she sat back and caught her own breath. Her canoe was very damp by this time for every tucanaré had brought in some of the Tapajoz River with it. She lifted her bare feet out of the wet and perched them on the canoe side. She tucked her line between her big toe and the next, and took her pipe out of her pocket. It was not a big man's pipe, like Papai's, which was made of imported briar. It was tiny, the bowl not bigger than Joa's thimble. And it held only a few grains of tobacco out of a little tobacco pouch a rubber tree had given her, as she told them later.

She had scarcely filled it and struck a match when Tatu saw her foot lift quickly. She reached for the line, and there was another fish. This one was quite a joke. It had insisted on being caught when she was not even fishing! And she had caught it with toes as clever as her fingers.

She looked up at Tatu laughing and saying her pole was magic. Tatu had better try it and give her a chance to smoke.

He must be quick as lightning, though, she said, handing up the pole.

Tatu had learned a lot from watching. But there was some trick even her pole would not do for him. He tried again and again. Mrs. Red-Skirt was a determined teacher, and kept him practicing long after she had finished her pipe-load of tobacco.

Meanwhile Tarzan had grown tired waiting for Joa to play with him, and had stirred up Guapo. The monkey and wild cat were chasing each other from one end of the deck to the other, tumbling against Joa so she could hardly go on with her fishing. They were making such an uproar that Alfredo came to see what was going on. Mamai had pulled her chair out of their way so that she could read in peace.

Guapo's fur was short but very thick. In fact it looked as if he were wearing a piece of handsome gray velvet carpet, instead of an animal's coat. And it was a good protection against Tarzan, who was trying to be nice and not too rough. But pretty soon Tarzan began to grow so wild and excited that he did not keep his claws in their sheaths. And he forgot not to bite too hard. His teeth finally went into Guapo's skin right through the thick fur.

Then Guapo bit back, with the strong teeth in his square jaws. Tarzan howled with surprise. Both animals ran away from each other and pretended that nothing had happened. They stood looking out at the scenery, while even Mamai laid down her book to laugh at them.

Alfredo tried Joa's line, and then pulled it in for her. Some passing fish had stolen her bait while she was on the other side of the boat. So he asked Mrs. Red-Skirt for one of her tucanaré since she had so many. And he used a piece of it to rebait Joa's hook. It was very fine bait that all river fish were hungry for, and Joa would surely catch a fine one now.

He started to go back to his quarters in the bow, when along came a giant grasshopper. It flew aboard and landed on the deck, with a flash of red wings. This kind of grasshopper is as big and heavy as a mouse. It is bright green above and scarlet underneath. Tatu had been hoping to catch one for his collection. But now he was too busy fishing even to see it.

Guapo spied it first with his quick monkey eyes, but Tarzan was the one who leaped after it. The grasshopper flew under Mamai's deck chair, and then the chase became a free-for-all, with both Guapo and Tarzan determined to be the one to catch the insect. The silly thing jumped from place to place, instead of flying away, with the two animals always nearly on top of it. But finally, when Tarzan actually had his paws on it, the grasshopper slipped out from under, spread its wide wings and started for shore, with Tarzan right behind. Through the rail Tarzan went, forgetting he had no wings. And he landed right in the river, while Guapo went bang into the railing and clung there grinning and chattering after his friend.

Mrs. Red-Skirt reached out her paddle but Tarzan floated down the current past her. Of course wildcats are good swimmers. But for a little fellow like Tarzan, the river was full of danger. In a second Mrs. Red-Skirt had loosened her rope and her canoe was shooting after him.

How she did paddle! She had to beat the current and reach the kitten before anything could happen to him. Tatu and Joa exclaimed as she passed him. But they understood the next second when she steadied her boat sidewise in his path, and reached for him as he dashed against the canoe's side.

She was just in time, for the head of a huge fish came up at that moment, and tried to grab Tarzan out of her hand. Tarzan would have made a nice meal for that fish. But he was safe in the canoe now, and being paddled back to his home.

He was a sorry looking kitty. His bright gold coat with its smart black leopard-spots was like a wet rag. His eyes were still popping out with fright, as Mrs. Red-Skirt passed him up into the launch. His legs wobbled and he shivered so he could scarcely stand. Guapo came to look at the wreck as if he did not even recognize his playmate. But Mamai was ready with a bath towel to wrap him in, all but his nose and eyes. She didn't care much for Tarzan, but he was so miserable that she held him on her lap and let him lick her finger for the first time. And no one could thank Mrs. Red-Skirt enough for saving their pet's life.

"It was nothing," insisted Mrs. Red-Skirt. "And now good-by. My children will be wondering what has happened to their tucanaré."

At that moment, Joa, who had idly taken up her pole again, shouted, "Oh, I've got a bite! Hold on to me!"

In fact, it looked as if she were about to be pulled over the rail into the river. Alfredo grabbed her. But Mrs. Red-Skirt did something more useful. She caught hold of Joa's line which was leaping about at a great rate over the canoe.

"Bring a boat hook! I think we've got the big fellow

Mrs. Red-Skirt steadied her boat and reached for Tarzan

who tried to gobble the cat!" she shouted. And Alfredo ran for his boat hook.

Slowly, a few inches at a time, Mrs. Red-Skirt pulled in the line. And soon glimpses of the fish were seen, as it tried to pull the fisherwoman and her canoe out into the stream. Its head and shoulders came out of the water, and it made a lash at her hand.

"Bacú!" she yelled to Alfredo. "Where's your hook?"

"Bacú! Look out!" shouted Alfredo, for the bacú is a very dangerous creature.

The next time the big fish came out of the water, Alfredo was ready with the long pole of the boat hook. No one ever knew how he had done it, for when he shouted, "Stand back!" they all ran for safety.

But there lay the great fish on the deck, with the boat hook beside it. And such a fish! It was literally covered with weapons, shears, swords, and dagger, all of them in action as it thrashed the deck. Two long stinging barbels grew out of its chin, and another out of the top of its tail. Its sharp front fins worked together exactly like a pair of scissors. Its head and shoulders were covered with armor plates of bone. And running down its back, from the armor to the tail, was a double-edged saw. Truly it was equipped to fight anything that swam in the river. And it was longer than Joa herself.

Alfredo kept yelling for them to keep out of the way unless they wished to lose an arm or a leg. But he kept saying proudly, too, that the beast must weigh forty pounds.

Mrs. Red-Skirt peeked over the edge of the deck, standing in her canoe to say good-by for sure this time. She said if she stayed any longer there was no telling what might happen.

Next time Joa would probably catch a whale.

Mamai laid down Tarzan and went to shake hands. Then they all saw that Mrs. Red-Skirt's hand was bleeding, from a small cut.

"Oh, that's nothing at all," she said. "Just fisherwoman's luck. I should have been more careful in a battle with a bacú."

But Mamai insisted on going to the cabin for the iodine bottle.

"Just keep on practicing, young man. You'll soon be a tucanaré expert," Mrs. Red-Skirt called back to Tatu as she paddled away. And Tatu promised he would.

The excitement had scarcely died down when Papai and Captain Santos were seen starting out from the river bank.

Tarzan had left the bath towel to lie in the sun, and Joa was brushing his tangled fur. The big fish lay still at last, for even a bacú can't live long out of water. Mamai was reading again, and Tatu had gone back to his practicing. But as soon as Papai stepped up on the launch, they all began talking at once, telling of the things that had happened that morning.

"What smells so sweet?" Mamai asked, suddenly, when there was a lull in the talk.

"Oh, I almost forgot!" exclaimed Papai. "I had an interesting morning, too. And I brought home something to prove it."

He began to unload his pockets. They were full of tonka beans which were giving off the sweet odor. He had found the tonka bean plantation back in the forest, where the great trees were growing wild. Although these trees were a hundred feet tall, they bore true beans, over an inch long, that looked as if they had been made of chocolate. And only one grew in each shell, which made them different from all other beans.

Of course no one thought of climbing the tall trees to pick them. They waited for the pods to ripen and be blown down by the wind. So the man who owned them might be said to have riches falling into his lap every time the wind blew.

Papai suggested that the children put some tonka beans in their suitcases, instead of sachets. He told them that in the United States and Europe the beans are turned into toilet water and perfumes. Also that bakers use them in vanilla and other flavoring extracts.

Just then another great grasshopper buzzed out from shore and landed with a loud plop right at Tatu's feet. The next second he had caught it under his hat before either Tarzan or Guapo could make a move. When the insect had been chloroformed in a big bottle, and mounted with its wings spread under a glass, Tatu thought it was one of his finest specimens.

The grasshopper made up somewhat to Tatu for his not being able to catch any tucanaré. But now Papai began to tease him and said that the trouble was that Tatu had not learned to hold the line with his toes and smoke a pipe. Papai took off one shoe, lighted his pipe and tied Tatu's line around his own toe to demonstrate. And a fish got fast to the hook right away. Tatu said Papai had this good luck because such a big school had come along and they were all so hungry. He could see a cloud of them swimming all around the boat.

"Then you try," said Papai, laying down the pole.

And sure enough, the minute the fly struck the water a

beautiful spotted beauty jumped for it. Tatu had three of them before the launch's motor began rattling and Captain Santos had her chugging up the river again, toward Itaituba, their last stop.

Tatu felt very proud as he carried his catch to Alfredo to grill over the charcoal fire. Alfredo already had bacú stew simmering in a big red earthen pot. But he said that could wait until supper.

It had been so much fun living on the launch that Tatu and Joa wished they could go on forever. Papai had said the Tapajoz River was a thousand miles long, so why couldn't they go on for a thousand miles?

Papai explained that would be lovely if there was any way for the launch to climb all the great waterfalls beyond Itaituba. Then they might travel far into the interior of the state of Mato Grosso and become real explorers. But the launch was not very good at going up waterfalls, so they would have to turn back toward home.

Itaituba turned out to be a charming place, although it was very small and far away from any other town. It consisted of one long row of houses, each built against the other, and painted pink. They sat on a high straight ridge above the river, with many doors looking out across a narrow green park and with great mango trees to give shade. Children were playing under the trees and sheep were grazing on the green. At least half the sheep were black and their little black lambs were adorable. They were such tame pets that they came right up to Tatu and Joa as if to ask who they were and where they had come from.

When the Amarals went into the store to shop, a pet monkey climbed out of his little hammock, trotted across the counter to inspect them and put out both his hands for them to shake. The storekeeper was delighted to see them, too. And as soon as the word got around, the whole town came to look at them. So few visitors ever came to Itaituba that they were really a great novelty. For that reason, too, there were no souvenirs for sale, such as could be bought in Santarem.

But, looking around, Tatu found a hammock for Guapo like the one the storekeeper had for his pet monkey. And Papai discovered some lovely colored river stones, some curious shells for the children's museum, and a wonderful stuffed alligator. The storekeeper sold them the monkey hammock and the alligator. But he wouldn't take any money for the stones and shells. They could have those to remember him by, he told them, and so they would not forget Itaituba.

XIII

Home Again

THE LAUNCH almost flew home, for the current had grown stronger since they went up the river a few days before.

"Why do we have to go so fast?" asked Joa. She didn't want the trip to end.

"Because the river is rising and the water is carrying us along," answered Captain Santos.

"But it hasn't rained for ever so long," said Tatu.

"Look at the sky. See those flying clouds?" Captain Santos' arm swept above his head. "That means the little rainy season is coming and it's already raining in some places. Besides, the snows are melting on the mountains far away."

"I wish it would pour." Mamai laid down her embroidery. "It's so hot even with the breeze blowing that I don't feel like doing anything."

"Oh, Senhora, you wouldn't like it if the first rains caught us here on the river." Captain Santos looked very seriously at the sky. "I'm only hoping that won't happen."

He kept watching the shore with his binoculars as he sat chatting with Papai after lunch, and finally got up, saying he had to look after things a bit.

The little clouds had disappeared and the heat shimmered above the water with scarcely a breath of air stirring. Mamai said it made her dizzy just to look at it. They kept creeping nearer and nearer to the river bank, too, where it was even more still and hot.

Presently Alfredo came to fasten down the little windows of the cabin, and tie the awnings tighter. He was making everything shipshape. He said Tatu and Joa had better pick up their things that were lying around and carry them inside.

He told them to be ready to go into the cabin at once when the squall began, for it might easily blow children overboard. He told them to take good care of themselves, for now he had to go help the Captain who was trying to reach the harbor of the rubber-ball maker for safety.

The wind blew in little puffs that twisted the hammocks and sent them flying. So Papai took them down. A spit of rain flashed across the floor. Tarzan and Guapo were already in hiding.

A big gust of wind came as Captain Santos guided the launch around the point into the little bay. It pushed them along straight toward the mouth of the creek. The creek had grown much wider with the rising flood of water. In fact it was running across the rubber man's front yard right into the door of his house. He had evidently gone away and had taken all his pots and other possessions with him. A flock of flamingoes, standing at the edge of his clearing, flew up like a house afire and disappeared in the forest. The Captain threw out the anchor and the launch rocked gently in the creek. All around were thick woods giving them shelter. They could see the wind sweeping up the river and raising little white caps. It was hot and quiet. Mamai fanned herself, and all sat waiting for something to happen.

They waited and waited.

After a while Captain Santos came back looking very pleased. The storm had passed over, for the present anyway.

Tatu and Joa were sorry. They were wanting some excitement.

And now the launch was skimming along again with the hot sun beating down. The passing squall had not cooled things off at all. And there was nothing much to do except look at the scenery.

The views were very pretty because the launch kept near the shore. The long beaches were not yet covered with water. Running along the edges of the white sands were pretty woods with tall palms and taller Brazil nut trees. And behind were the rolling sandy lands that led up to the high blue hills in the distance. Every minute the scenery changed, and, of course, that helped to make it interesting.

Next day Santarem came in sight, and shortly they were stopping in front of their own sandy beach. But the first thing they noticed was that the edge of the river had moved up until it was almost touching the log where Maria did her washing.

The house looked nice and cool and peaceful. No one was in sight except Peixe-Boi, standing alone and looking very bored in front of the veranda steps.

Captain Santos sounded his horn, which was a real horn that had once grown on a cow. Maria came to the door, and then Alzira. They stood there smiling and waving, and both ran down to the river. Peixe-Boi came lumbering after them. And Perla and Boy could be heard screaming welcomes from their veranda perch.

"Where's José?" was Tatu's first question.

"He went with his grandfather this morning to hunt for their canoe," Maria told him. "It got loose in the night and floated away."

All the Amarals were sorry about that, for a canoe in Santarem is more useful than a team of oxen.

"Oh, I do hope they find it," said Mamai, thinking of the times Sr. Diogo had taken her down town in it to save her walking.

"When are they coming back?" asked Papai.

"They have to be back for the milking in the morning. The cows had their grass. And we said we would feed them their salted cottonseed tonight, and let the calves in to have their supper."

"Did Sr. Diogo and José walk?" Tatu was wishing he had been here in time to go along.

"No. They borrowed my father's canoe," exclaimed Maria. "That's another reason they have to hurry back, for my father needs it."

Meanwhile all the things had been unloaded from the launch and carried to the front steps. And the Amarals had said good-by to Captain Santos and Alfredo who were wanting to see their families now.

With every package and bundle that was brought to the veranda, Perla had become more and more excited. She surely was glad to see them. And now Mamai and Papai sat down to rest and told the children they would have to be quiet and cool off after their trips with the luggage back and forth in the hot sun. Then Perla, with such a good audience after the house had been quiet for so long, really began to show off.

She started making them a political speech. Maria said this was one of Perla's best performances. She had learned it when she belonged to a politician down the river, who had practiced all his campaign oratory in front of her. But she would do it only on special occasions, such as this, when the family came back from a journey.

Perla began quietly enough, addressing them as "Friends and Fellow Voters." At first she talked in the sweetest tones. She stood quite still on her perch, her head cocked so she could look at them with one eye, the way parrots do.

When she saw they were all interested, including Tarzan and Guapo, she grew louder and swayed from one claw to the other. Then she really warmed up to her subject. She ruffled her feathers, flapped her wings, and leaped up and down. She screamed and shouted in her most raucous voice, and went on and on. Of course, no one could understand a word she was trying to say, except once in a while when she interrupted herself with, "Viva Brazil! Hurrah for our Democratic Party!"

It was a very funny act, and the more they laughed the more Perla performed.

Meanwhile, Boy was eying her jealously. He sidled closer and closer until he left her almost no room for leaping about. And finally he gave her a hard peck on the head which stopped the speech off short.

"Oh!" she gurgled. "Oh—oh!" It hurt but she didn't peck back.

Instead she began reciting a poem in a low voice so as not to bother Boy. He seemed to approve of that. It was something about friendship. And then she burst into a song, a jingling tune that Boy tried to join. But she raced along so fast that he could not keep up with her. Altogether her show was running down. So the Amarals clapped long and loud, and that ended it.

Tatu and Joa could hardly wait toward the last, for they wanted so much to see Branquissimo and Jasmina, and all the other pets.

The parakeets, Cap, the jabotis, and especially the horses were so glad they were home again. Even the wild birds crowded around—all begging, for José had had to hurry away without feeding them.

Of course there was not enough corn, because Maria and Alzira had been busy helping with Sr. Diogo's chores. And Tatu and Joa had to pull off the shucks and shell a lot of ears. But they let Branquissimo and Jasmina, and also Cap, with his scissors teeth, shell their own. For by this time Tatu's arms ached and Joa's hands were scratched with the rough husks.

They piled a dozen husked ears in each horse manger, and watched the dainty way Jasmina and Branquissimo nibbled at the grains until the ears were only corncobs, then picked up with their lips all the grains that had dropped.

After that the children visited the calves who were hungry, too, and crying to be let in with their mothers. Maria said they could take down the bars between the calf pen and the cows' corral. So now everybody was happy, including Tatu and Joa, who were thinking how very nice it was to be home again in Santarem.

Sr. Diogo and José got back after midnight. When Papai heard the paddles he got up to see them pulling their borrowed canoe out of the water.

"Did you find it?" he called out.

Sr. Diogo looked up surprised to see Papai at the hammock-room door. He shook his head, and then came wearily across the beach with José beside him. They were both tired, for they had traveled as fast and as far as they could since early morning. No one along the river had seen a runaway canoe. Anyway it was like looking for a needle in a haystack, since there were a million little inlets and creeks where it could have landed, especially now, with the river rising. At next low water someone might find it. Or maybe it had gone all the way to Belem and out into the Atlantic Ocean.

Tatu waked up to hear Sr. Diogo telling the story, and Papai saying it was hard luck.

"Yes, it is bad luck," Sr. Diogo agreed sadly, "for there is never a canoe for sale in all Santarem. People always make their own, and usually they last them a life time."

Then he said good night, for he had to snatch an hour's sleep before waking up to do the milking at three o'clock. People would be waiting for their coffee and chocolate, and José would have to help deliver the milk for them no matter how sleepy and tired he was.

José grinned at Tatu, who was peeking over the edge of the hammock, wide awake.

Tatu had made up his mind he would not go to sleep again. When three o'clock came he would be ready to help Sr. Diogo strain and bottle the milk. And then he would go out with José and the bottles at dawn. He would fix up a pannier on Branquissimo's saddle to hold them. Branquissimo was so gentle he wouldn't mind working like a pack mule just once. He wouldn't be frightened at the bottles rattling on his back either. Tatu's head was full of plans.

But before he knew it, he opened his eyes and it was bright morning with the sun shining outside. He had gone to sleep in spite of his good intentions.

He leaped out in his pajamas and ran to the kitchen. Alzira said the milking was over long ago. And José had been gone so long it was almost time for him to come back to his breakfast.

Tatu felt badly about that. And he was quite angry with himself because he had gone to sleep so easily. He said nothing to anyone, not even to Joa. But he jumped into his clothes, threw the bridle over Branquissimo's head and started off bareback to meet José.

José, being young, had the easiest milk route, nearest the dairy. So Tatu did not have to hunt long to find him. In fact, José was sitting under a mango tree in the nearest public square. Near by were his two baskets of empty bottles. Beside him lay the pole that went across his shoulders and carried the baskets.

He had finished and was resting before starting back. He smiled up at Tatu. His smile grew brighter when Tatu said he and Branquissimo had come to help. Then Tatu blurted out that he had intended to stay awake, but hadn't been able to.

José said he couldn't have done that himself, especially when it was dark. Why, Sr. Diogo always had to shake him awake every morning. But his grandfather, having been a sailor, could jump out of bed any minute and never mind at all.

Tatu slid off Branquissimo and led him to a low wall. They balanced the basket of bottles on his shoulders. Tatu climbed up and held them steady, then José with the pole got up behind. Branquissimo kept looking around at his strange load, but Tatu explained it to him. And he also told the horse to go home without guiding, for it was hard enough to hold onto the baskets, let alone the bridle.

Branquissimo seemed to understand. At any rate, he stepped carefully and walked straight toward the beach and then right up to the veranda.

Maria threw up her hands. She had hunted everywhere for Tatu to give him his breakfast. But she never thought to look for Branquissimo. She might have known, she said, that the horse and Tatu would have been together.

Then Mamai, who had been unpacking, came out onto the veranda with the gifts from their trip. She and Papai had remembered everybody when they were visiting Mr. Ford's store at the rubber plantations, which sold many things from North America.

There were presents for Maria, Alzira and Sr. Diogo. José was given the smallest flashlight he had ever seen, with a clip to fasten it into his pocket. There was a Scout knife for

Tomás and new hair ribbons for Sara. And at that moment,
who should appear in the distance but these two children,
waving, coming to say hello and play awhile.

Mamai brought a card for Tatu to write to John and Margaret. It would go in the box with the rubber balls that she
was sending back by mail to the Ford plantation. Tatu hurried to finish before Tomás and Sara could arrive. "Remem-
brances from Tatu," he wrote. Then he added, "and Joa," for,
after all, his sister didn't have anything to send.

His mother looked at the card and showed it to Joa. She
was smiling happily because Tatu had been so thoughtful.

XIV

Building a Canoe

SENHOR DIOGO had to have a new canoe. The two grass cutters from across the river offered to work a few days and help make it. So they stayed one morning after bringing over the food for the cows, and talked it over. Their names were Pedro and Antonio.

They knew of just the right tree in the woods near by. They described the tree and where it grew; a yellow ironwood, strong as steel and not too heavy. Sr. Diogo had seen it, too. He agreed with them. Nothing could be better.

Pedro and Antonio said they could cut it down by themselves, even if the two of them couldn't bring it out afterward. So, why not commence right now?

José and Tatu were listening, because it sounded very interesting. They were afraid the men would think them too small to be of any use for such a heavy job. But they did want to watch, at least.

When they asked Sr. Diogo he said they could go along, if they would keep out of the men's way. He always wanted José to learn how to do everything. But they must be sure not to get lost as they had before, in that same jungle, when they were hunting for Bonequinho. Sr. Diogo told them never to go out of hearing of the axes and machetes.

Both boys promised.

The men walked down the beach carrying their tools. The boys followed with a large gourd, full of pure water to drink. For tree-chopping is thirsty work.

Joa was playing on the veranda. She never looked up as they skirted the kitchen path. Tatu was hoping she wouldn't notice, for surely she would want to come with them, if she knew what was going on.

When they reached the woods they turned into the same path Sr. Diogo and the boys had come from, after the Bonequinho hunt. In a few minutes they reached the yellow ironwood tree, which was not far inside the jungle.

The first thing to be done was to clear away a place for the tree to fall. The growth is so thick in these Brazilian forests, and there are so many tough vines, that a tree will stand up a long time even after it has been cut in two.

The men walked around the tree, then planned to lay it down on the side where there were no other big trees to keep it from falling. They cut down the little trees and cleared away all the undergrowth with their machetes.

Then they went to work on the ironwood trunk. Ironwood was a good name for it because it was so hard that only small chips fell each time the axes struck. But, little by little, the notch in the trunk grew bigger. Every once in awhile, Antonio and Pedro would stand off and look at it, to make sure the tree would fall where they wanted it. They stopped only long enough to take big drinks of water.

Tatu and José sat on two stones in a safe place beside the

trail. It was fun, for they didn't know when the tree was going to topple over.

"Now!" Antonio shouted.

"Look out!" grunted Pedro, as his ax hit deep beyond the tree's heart.

When the trunk bent ever so little, they both leaped aside. It seemed to wait a moment, then leaned gently over, farther and farther. Suddenly it came down with a crash.

"Within six inches of the spot!" boasted Pedro.

"It couldn't have been better!" said Antonio, examining the cut. They were much pleased, and showed Tatu and José how even and regular they had made the ax marks.

In the branches of the fallen tree, though, was something even more interesting to Tatu. Gleaming out of the green was a large white wasp's nest, the kind he had been searching for in every tree top since he had come to Santarem. And this one looked new and perfect. It hadn't even been hurt by the tree's falling.

He started for it, opening his pocket knife. But Antonio stopped him.

"Don't go too near," he said. "Maybe there are live wasps inside. They can sting you to death if they take the notion. Wait until tomorrow after they leave and we'll get it out for you."

Tatu knew that wasps always abandon a nest after it has been torn down. He couldn't see any going in and out the door even now. But he didn't want to be stung, so he wisely decided to wait, as Antonio said.

Pedro and Antonio now measured off a log twenty feet long, and started cutting away the upper part of the trunk at that spot. It was round and smooth and very straight.

That part of the work was not so interesting to watch, so José and Tatu decided to walk around a bit.

"This looks like the old pig track," said José, leaning over and peering through the brush.

"It is the old pig track. Here's my handkerchief still tied to this bush!" exclaimed Tatu. "Only it's awfully dirty and full of spider webs."

"Maybe we can find our circus tent. Let's look for it," José's black eyes shone.

"And get lost again?" Tatu was thinking of their promise to Sr. Diogo.

"No, we won't. Listen to the axes!" At that José started off down the track. "It looks exactly like the place."

"What if we meet the pigs?" suggested Tatu.

"No pigs or any other animals hang around when they hear woodsmen working. They're deep in the jungle by now— Oh, come on! Don't be such a fraidy cat!"

So Tatu followed along, thinking he shouldn't. And all at once the noise of chopping stopped.

José stopped, too. He looked a little scared. And Tatu said, "What did I tell you?"

José made a trumpet of his hands and hallooed. He called in all directions. Then a yell came back almost beside them. Antonio and Pedro were only a few feet away. Antonio called to them to stand still, and the two machetes could be heard chopping out a path. In a few minutes the men walked through the jungle curtain, swinging their big knives.

They said they had finished cutting off the log, and that it was time for lunch. It had taken them the whole morning, and they were not going to do any more until tomorrow.

"So, we didn't get lost, did we?" whispered José.

Tatu shook his head.

"I know just where the circus tent is, now," said José. "Let's come again tomorrow."

"What are you two whispering about?" asked Pedro.

"About coming again tomorrow morning," José answered.

"All right, if you want to," said Pedro. "We'll need a pair of good water carriers."

By the next day several more friends of Sr. Diogo had volunteered to drag the log out of the woods. They came early, and when all started out together it looked like a picnic party. Alzira had made a refreshing drink out of palm fruits, which she poured into gourds for Tatu and José to carry. She even handed Joa a smaller gourd to take along. For Joa was not being left out this time. And Tatu was glad of that. He felt guilty after slipping away from her yesterday.

Sr. Diogo had bought some mandioca cakes and sweet rolls in town in case they grew hungry doing all the hard work. He led the procession. He thought the ironwood log was beautiful the minute he saw it.

While the others went to find and cut some very strong vines to use as ropes, Sr. Diogo, Antonio and Pedro chopped the trunks of little trees into short lengths. They were going to use these as rollers.

Finally, when everything was ready, a dozen rollers were laid in place on the path, and the log was turned over on them. The vine ropes were tied to it. Some of the men walked in front and at the side and pulled the ropes. Two of them pushed the log from behind and others kept clearing the path.

The log traveled head on, but only a few feet at a time. When a roller was left behind, someone picked it up and laid it in front, so it could begin rolling all over again.

This was very tedious and the children soon grew tired of seeing the log creeping along so slowly. Then José remembered his plan to find the circus tent. It would be a wonderful place to play.

Now, there were no axes to listen to, only the voices of the men, calling out when all should pull together.

Tatu said, "We'll show Joa what is in the woods, but let's not go too far."

José thought he knew these woods very well by this time. It was Joa who was skipping along ahead, very excited to be exploring.

Pretty soon they came to a little babbling brook that ran down into the pig's pond.

"Oh, look!" Joa dropped to her knees on a rock beside a tiny waterfall. "I see gold!"

The boys were on their knees beside her, and all three of them were gazing into the water at the white sand underneath, where flakes of pure gold danced in the sun. They looked at each other with big eyes. Here were riches. But how could they get hold of them?

"If only we had a tin pan we could be placer miners," said Tatu. "I saw a movie once where miners were doing it. They dip up water and dirt in the pan and swirl it around. The gold goes to the bottom and they pour off the rest."

"But we haven't got a pan," said José.

"How about those banana leaves over there?" Joa pointed.

They pulled off a few wild banana leaves and found them too soft to serve as pans. So they laid the leaves on the sloping bank, scooped up the sands with their hands, and poured it into the leaves.

The water ran off. They picked out the gold flakes with their fingers and laid them on a dry spot. Soon Joa went down the stream a few feet and found an even better place. They worked hard, quiet as mice. Not far away they could hear the men singing out,

"Ready— Pull!" "Ready— Pull!" "Again, ready— Pull!"

Soon each of the miners had a tiny pile of shining gold. Then they had to quit, for Sr. Diogo was calling them. They tore off bits of banana leaf, wrapped up their riches, and hid them away in their pockets. They were not going to tell a soul—only Papai, who knew everything. He could teach them about gold mining, and they would be millionaires.

By this time the log was lying on the beach at the river's edge. It was ready to push into the water and be floated home. Beside it was Tatu's big white wasps' nest, which he was told again not to touch.

Sr. Diogo was handing out cakes to everybody resting in the shade. He asked the children to pass the gourds of palm drink. It was a nice ending to a strenuous morning.

When Papai came home that night, the log had been dragged to high ground under a big shady tree. There it lay on trestles, and the work of hollowing it out had already begun. Everybody helped at this, telling Sr. Diogo that many hands make light work. They took turns with chisels and hammers, first making a slit down the whole length. Then, reaching through this long narrow opening, they removed the inside of the log. It was a patient job that would take them nearly a week.

Even Papai had never seen a canoe being made. He was much interested and asked many questions. He didn't yet know what important news the children had to tell him. Joa kept pulling at his sleeve, trying to attract his attention. He would reach out to pinch her ear, or give her a pat, and go on talking. She thought he was never going to stop and listen to her.

But finally he did.

"What's this? A secret? What kind of a secret?" Papai spoke quite loud. Tatu whispered, "Sh-sh-sh—" And José crowded near to hear what Joa would say next.

"Come out to the quintal with us. Please do, Papai. We'll tell you there."

She took him by the hand and led him along. Papai was looking very serious, by this time. But his eyes were smiling. He thought this was some new kind of game.

Joa never stopped until they came to Jasmina's stall, where no one could see them from the house. Then she felt in her pocket for her little banana leaf package of gold. The boys took theirs out, too, while Tatu explained how they had found it in the creek, and no one else knew about it but them. Jasmina looked around at them, pricking up her ears and wrinkling her nose with the greatest interest.

Papai took each package in turn and carefully examined it.

"It's real gold, Papai," Tatu insisted. "It's exactly like what I saw in the movies one time. We are going to take pans

out to the woods and pan it just like real miners do. You'll
show us how, won't you, Papai?"

Papai was pursing up his lips and looking very doubt-
ful.

"First I'll get some acid from the house and we'll test it
before making plans," he said. "You wait here."

He came back with a little bottle and a bit of plate glass.
He laid a few gold flakes on the glass. He took out the stop-
per of the bottle and put a drop of acid on each gold flake.
The acid foamed up and the gold disappeared.

"That's what I was afraid of," said Papai. "Your gold is
only iron pyrites. It's 'fool's gold,' and you were well fooled."

"Are you sure, Papai?" Tatu could hardly believe it.

"Very sure! You see, real gold is not affected by this acid

at all. In fact, gold is almost indestructible. That's one of the reasons it is so valuable."

Tatu and Joa were looking so sad that Papai felt sorry.

"Never mind," he said. "Some day I'll take you to a place where there really is gold, and let you mine some of it."

Soon, in the excitement of making the canoe, they forgot their disappointment. Visitors were always there, and every day the canoe was different.

At last it was all hollowed out, but the sides were not wide enough for anyone to ride in it. The most important part was still to be done, and that consisted of stretching it until the empty log would be shaped like a boat.

This was very tricky, and Sr. Diogo wouldn't trust anyone but himself to add this finishing touch. No one else wanted to do it, either. For if a mistake were made now the whole log might accidentally split in two and all the hard work would be lost.

Sr. Diogo turned it over, with the open side down. It was light and easy to move now, with all its insides gone. Then he built a long fire under it. As soon as the green wood was warm and softened by the heat, he stuck boards across inside and pounded in wedges at the ends of these boards to stretch the opening. This had to be done very gently and carefully. The fires were kept going all day long. And every so often, Sr. Diogo would put in longer boards, or bigger wedges, especially in the middle. Gradually the sides belled out. He kept watch constantly. If the tiniest crack appeared, he eased the wedges. Luckily, it turned out well without a split in it. And that was fine, said Sr. Diogo.

The fires died down, and slowly the canoe cooled off. By

the next evening the boards and wedges were removed and it was ready to try out.

Quite a crowd gathered. The boat was turned right side up. Seats were fastened in it and it was decorated with streamers and flowers and a Brazilian banner in the stern. The men bore it on their shoulders in triumph and launched it in the water, while all clapped and shouted.

Joa and Tatu had been invited to take the first ride. They sat proudly up in the bow with José behind them, and Sr. Diogo, Antonio and Pedro did the paddling. They paddled up and down many times, to show how light the craft floated, and how true and straight she was. On shore, people were applauding and Papai was sending up rockets and shooting off fire crackers.

Altogether it was a lovely celebration. And it finished with a real party, for Papai had bought refreshments including ice-cream, which arrived just as the canoe landed on the beach.

XV

A Wonderful Day

Papai had insisted that Tatu put his wasps' nest in a big biscuit tin with a large wad of cotton soaked in chloroform, before trying to handle it. That would finish off any young wasps which might be getting ready to fly. Tatu was tired of waiting but now at last he could examine it thoroughly.

The nest was wonderfully made. Never had insects invented a prettier home. It was cone-shaped, with the pointed end of the cone built around a branch. And it was about a foot and a half long. In fact, Tarzan could have slept in it very comfortably if he could have got in. But the wasps had built it so nothing larger than themselves could enter the door at the flat end. This door was a perfect circle, and was smooth and neat. Tatu could see a little hall just inside that led to hundreds of tiny chambers which were the nurseries of the wasp babies.

And the whole thing was built of paper pulp. If the mother wasps had chewed up fine writing paper it couldn't have turned out whiter or more beautiful. In fact, as Tatu was admiring it, he was thinking that maybe Papai would get one of the Santarem artists to paint a picture on it. They often made water-color sketches on such nests, for the smooth paper was so tempting. Tatu thought an orchid would be pretty, painted with a big blue butterfly poised above it. He would have liked to try painting it himself, but was afraid he would spoil it.

Wasps were surely marvelous builders. They could do things which men could not imitate. Even when they used common mud in other kinds of nests they were real architects. Tatu was becoming very much interested in them. And he remembered that he had intended to look at what had been going on in the upper corner of the veranda. A swarm had been making a terrific noise up there, buzzing and humming. Mamai was afraid of them until Sr. Diogo said that if she didn't bother wasps they wouldn't bother her.

Now Tatu climbed up with his magnifying glass to see what he could see. The first thing he discovered was that there were two kinds of wasps working there, each building its own sort of house. Both kinds were quite tame and didn't seem to mind having a visitor. In fact, they seemed to prefer staying around people's homes to living in the jungle like the paper builders.

One kind was black and nearly an inch long. And it made the most noise, so when several of these were working at the same time it was a miniature orchestra playing. The ones just arriving zoomed across the veranda with a loud ho-hum. When one of them went to work, she took a little ball of moist gray clay out of her mouth and laid it on the edge of her cell. Then with her lips and mandibles, or jaws, she spread the clay evenly, all the time singing her busy song, buzzing more quietly. Tatu, watching through the lens, could see her lower lips working, and her feet patting down the damp layer until she was satisfied with it. Then she would fly off for another tiny pill of clay. At this rate it would take her days to erect one small chamber about three inches long. But wasps are patient creatures, Tatu decided.

The other kind of wasp, which was less noisy, was also smaller. It came rushing home with the same happy hum, though it sang in a softer key. And its nests were the most curious little things. Each was the shape of a squat jug with a tiny neck and flaring mouth. These little jugs were set side by side in a straight neat row. One had just been finished. And Tatu watched a mother wasp bring back a small caterpillar and tuck it into this nest. Then she placed an egg inside. The caterpillar had been made unconscious by the wasp's sting, Tatu knew, and would stay that way to serve as food for the baby when it hatched out. After that the mother brought more clay and sealed up the opening.

Tatu climbed down deciding that insects were the most interesting creatures in the world, and that he had been neglecting his collection for too long a time.

"Sister!" he shouted at Joa, who was just starting off on Jasmina. "How would you like to go bug hunting?"

"All right," Joa answered, "if you'll stop for an ice at the Mascotte— I've got the money—" She had just been wondering what she would do this afternoon.

"Then wait for me!"

Tatu was back on Branquissimo in a minute with his bug-hunting outfit fastened to the saddle. And Mamai, who had heard them, came out as she always did to call good-by, and to warn them not to be late for supper.

As they rode toward the Mascotte on the beach which was growing narrower every day, Tatu remembered a long tongue of sand, running out into the Tapajoz beyond the town, where he had seen some strange insects working. Or maybe they had been little sand crabs. He would soon find out, he told Joa, for that was where they were going now.

The spit of sand was much shorter than it was when he saw it before, because the river was rising. But it was still long enough so they could look up and down the stream for miles. And the little creatures were still working. Spurts of sand were shooting up here and there.

"Those are just digger crabs," announced Joa.

"I don't think so," said Tatu, sitting down by the side of one of the sand fountains.

Joa knelt beside him and they both watched. Presently the sand stopped and out of the hole where it had been shooting, something moved. First a round green part appeared, then legs and a head, for it was backing out.

"A wasp!" exclaimed Tatu. "Another kind of wasp!" as the little thing walked around the edge of her nest inspecting. Then she rose in the air, took a few turns to make sure she could find it again, and flew away.

Meanwhile another mamma wasp had landed near by and was looking around for a choice spot. Tatu had his pocket lens ready. But the insect was so busy that it didn't bother her at all.

"See all the bristles up and down her front legs!" Tatu handed the magnifying glass to Joa.

"Are those what she stings with? Oh, I'm afraid she'll come after me!" Joa drew back.

"No, she digs with them. And she doesn't want to bother with you either. Watch her getting busy."

Her front feet moved so fast they were just a blur. The sand splattered until she disappeared, then it came out in a neat jet, until she had a little tunnel two or three inches deep.

She had scarcely finished and flown away, when the first wasp was back. Through the magnifying glass they saw she was hugging a numbed fly.

"See?" whispered Tatu. "She's carrying it down her own tunnel where she'll lay her egg on it."

They both watched the hole closely, and soon she came out, backward. She used her front feet next to shovel sand over the hole, and finally she smoothed it off so no one could see she had ever been there. Then she was ready to dig another.

Joa had been interested in this homemaking even though she was afraid of being stung.

And now Tatu said he had had enough of wasps for one morning, especially since they were too dangerous to catch. He would hunt something else for a change. He didn't have to go far. The whole place was swarming and buzzing with bugs of one sort and another.

Soon he spied a splash of golden carpet near the water.

"Look, Joa! Gold!" Tatu pointed. "Only that's not 'fool's gold.'"

The splash of bright carpet was a big flock of yellow butterflies, the same kind Tatu had seen at the rubber-ball maker's hut. He remembered how they had flown away over the water in a cloud before he could get his net. So this time he was going to sneak up on them.

He warned Joa to stand where she was, and not to make a sound or a motion. With his net lifted, he crept nearer and nearer, one step at a time.

The butterflies had landed on a spot of wet gray clay at the edge of the water. Their wings were folded, and they were absolutely still. Evidently they were sipping something good they had found on the clay. If Tatu had not seen this same kind before, he would have thought they were flowers blooming there.

By being very patient and slow, he came near enough, at last. Then he made a quick dash and caught a netful, many more than he could take care of. He kept only six, and popped them into the chloroforming bottle. When he let the rest go, they swarmed together, and hurried to catch up with their brothers, who were flying near the water and making for the other shore, several miles away.

This was a favorite place for butterflies to settle and drink, for animals and people seldom came here to frighten them. And soon, walking cautiously along the edge of the water, Joa exclaimed over another patch of color. This time it was green-gilt, and proved to be a swarm of smaller butterflies sitting on the damp sands with their wings spread wide open. They glittered like jewels in the sunlight. It was no trouble at all to catch some of them.

After that Tatu netted a big fellow, black with red lines and green spots, and two long painted tails growing out of its back wings.

He was going to keep on, he said, until he had a complete collection of every butterfly which flies in Santarem. That would be a lot of work, for he had heard there were more than eighty kinds altogether. But this would be a wonderful spot to hunt them.

"You aren't going to do it now, are you, Tatu?" asked Joa a little crossly.

"Of course not. It's going to take days to get them all."

"You said you'd go to the Mascotte with me," Joa reminded him.

Tatu laughed, because Joa's appetite was a family joke. But really she ate less than he did himself, and only about half as much as Papai. He looked at the sun. It would soon touch the edge of the sky.

"All right, Sis," he said. "Come on! Only I want to ride to town by the back way, and find out where some of these butterflies come from."

Going back toward town, they were walking the horses through a deep sandy path, when Joa suddenly cried out and reined in Jasmina.

"Oh, Tatu! How awful!" Joa's voice sounded shivery. She was leaning over Jasmina's neck, staring down at something, her eyes as big as saucers.

Tatu thought it must be a snake, until he had a good look at it. Instead it was a toad sitting in the narrow road. Even then he didn't laugh, as he usually did at Joa's fears, for this toad was a monster, the biggest one he had ever seen. It was nearly a foot long. And he couldn't tell how high it was, for it was squatting as flat as possible, hoping not to be seen. Jasmina's hooves were almost on it, and she was backing away of her own accord.

Maybe it was dead, he thought, sliding out of the saddle. But it was very much alive. Its big sides were breathing, and its cold eyes looked at him crossly. He pushed at it with his shoe. It felt soft and heavy. But it didn't stir an inch.

"Be careful, Tatu!" Joa warned. "You'll get warts."

"Toads don't make warts, silly. That's just a superstitious idea," answered Tatu.

"But they do. I've always heard that. And they breath poison on you, too."

Tatu wanted to pick up the beast, as he had picked up little ones many a time, and show Joa how wrong she was. But really he was a little bit afraid of it himself. Instead he went back over the path and found a good strong stick.

He worked the stick into the sand underneath the toad while Joa was gasping and begging him to let it alone, and then he used all his strength to hoist the creature into the air. It fell on the side of the path with a plop. But instead of leaping away, it slowly turned around and sat up at last, its ugly head lifted above its long front legs. It glared as if it would like to eat them both if it could. Why should they come bothering a poor defenseless animal on his own grounds? They should stay in the town, where they belonged.

"See him now, Joa! He certainly would spit poison at us if he could. I made him awfully mad."

"But you saved his life. Jasmina surely would have trampled on him."

"I don't think so. Horses don't like to kill things and they have very sharp eyes and keen noses. Jasmina would have stepped over him if you hadn't stopped her and so would Branquissimo. But I didn't think about that then."

"What made him act so queer? What was he doing there, anyway?"

"All toads act like that. They are the color of the ground, so they think if they keep quiet they are invisible. You pass lots of them without seeing them."

Just then a swarm of flying ants swooped down around the toad's head. They surely did not see him. Out shot his sticky tongue to be covered with insects. It moved in and out like a machine. He had a fine meal before they became frightened and flew away.

"And that was what he was doing, Joa—waiting for his supper to walk into his mouth."

"Ugh!" Joa made a face. "I really think you like that old toad."

Tatu nodded. "Maybe I do—a little."

"Why don't you chloroform him then, and put him in your bug collection?" Joa giggled at her good joke as they rode away. And Tatu thought it was pretty funny, too.

As they sat on the terrace of the Mascotte, they watched the beaches swarming with people coming down for their evening baths. Many went into their palm-leaf bath houses, instead of into the river. But others walked into the water, poking the bottom with sticks in front of them. Long ago Sr. Diogo had rebuilt their bathhouse, and made it so strong Peixe-Boi couldn't push it over. This very morning Maria had said for them to take "gourd" baths in there, because of the sting rays in the river. And now the bathers who wanted a swim were certainly being careful.

Maybe, at last, Tatu would have a chance to see one of those terrible water monsters. He was hoping so.

And sure enough, as they neared home, fishermen were still at work, even though it was growing dusk. Fish had been hard to catch today. And one of the men sang out to Tatu. He dangled a kite-shaped thing in the air.

"A sting ray for your museum, Tatu! What do you think of it?"

"It doesn't look very different from any other skate, does it?" Tatu turned it around, for it was dead and not dangerous any longer. "That is, except for its tail," he added, and shivered a little, for the tail was really frightening. It was a long whip of jointed bone, very sharp on the end, and full of jagged points. Toward the tip was the stinger, hinged to the side, and working like one blade of a pair of scissors. It had a row of teeth on either edge, like a two-sided saw. One row pointed one way, and the other row pointed in the opposite direction. Thus it wouldn't fail to cut deep into anything it touched.

The fisherman unhinged the sting and gave it to Tatu, telling him to be careful in handling it. And Tatu was so pleased he hardly knew how to express his thanks.

Truly this had been a wonderful collecting day.

XVI

Joa Has an Idea

GUAPO HAD ALWAYS thought it was very nice to live on the back porch railing. He could see everything that went on in the kitchen and quintal. And the family were always stopping to pet him and give him bananas, his favorite fruit. It was better than it had been in the jungle, where he had to hunt his own bananas.

But after his trip up the Tapajoz he seemed to hate his leash and wanted to be with the children all the time. He was always calling to Tatu, who would stop anything he was doing to let the monkey ride on his shoulder.

And now Perla seemed to think Nene and Pepe were nearly grown up. She didn't come to see them so often, to groom their feathers and tend to their manners. So they were often bored and climbed up to ride on Tatu's other shoulder. Papai said all Tatu needed was a hand-organ and a fortune-telling outfit. Then he could go to all the fairs with his pets and make a lot of money.

Joa laughed when Papai said that. She thought Guapo would love to pass a cup for coins, and the parakeets could easily learn to pick cards out of a box. But while she was laughing, suddenly she had an idea, and she could hardly wait to tell it to Tatu.

She would make a little suit and cap for Guapo. They would buy the fortunes out of their allowances, or they could even make them. All the cards ever said was, "You will gain riches," or, "You will marry the man of your choice," or, "Your enemy is a blond woman,"—things like that. And maybe she could teach Tarzan to jump through a hoop! They would train the animals and have a fair of their own.

Tatu thought Joa had a grand idea. And he was all for keeping it a secret from Papai and Mamai. How could that be done, though?

It would be easy, Joa said. She could do her sewing at the end of the quintal where Papai and Mamai never went. She would keep her things in Jasmina's stall which was big, like a room. And Tatu could give the pets their lessons at the same time, under the horses' shed. If Maria happened to see them, when she was roasting coffee, or catching a chicken for dinner, she wouldn't tell, if they asked her not to. Oh, it was going to be lots of fun!

First they had to ride downtown to do their shopping. Fortunately Joa had some money. Tatu spent every tostão for curios as fast as he got them. But Joa saved. She had a little pottery bank, a rooster with a slot in his back. He rattled nicely with the coins inside, but they wouldn't come out after ever so much patient shaking. She had to break him open, which was too bad, for he was quite pretty. She and Tatu carried the bank out into the garden and smashed it on a rock. Even Joa was surprised that she had saved so much.

They would train the animals and have a fair

There would be plenty for everything.

Joa borrowed Mamai's tapeline and measured Guapo. It tickled, and the monkey held onto the line when she was through. He laughed and chattered, and he wouldn't let go until she had opened every one of his fingers.

In town the storekeeper took down all the bright-colored stuff he had, bolts and bolts of it. At first the children couldn't make up their minds between polka dots and checks, but finally they agreed on some red-checked gingham. When the merchant heard Joa saying she wanted only a few inches, he smiled broadly. He said he thought he was selling them at least a few yards. But that Joa must be buying a dress for her doll.

Tatu said yes, it was going to be something like a doll's dress.

Next they went to the market. And there they found the most adorable straw hat for Guapo. It was intended for an ornament and was just the right size for his little head. This would be much better than a cap. A market man was just coming in with a load of baskets from the country. And fortunately some of them were small. Tatu picked out one with a handle and a design in red for Guapo to take up the collection instead of using a tin cup.

They were just leaving the market with their packages, when whom should they meet but Papai!

"What have you got there? What have you two been up to?" Of course he had to ask them.

"It's a secret," said Joa.

"Oh, you've been finding more gold mines, I see," he said, pinching Joa's cheek and grinning.

But fortunately he had to hurry over to the bank to meet a man. And he forgot to tease them about it afterward.

When they went home, José was there. After he had heard all about the scheme, he was as excited as they were, and he was very proud when Joa said they wanted him to be in it, too, if he would be sure not to let his grandfather know anything about it. José promised. He put his hand on his heart saying, "Let an alligator eat me, if ever I breathe a word to anybody!" And that was as strong a promise as he could make.

He said he had a good idea for his part. He had kept his old carnival costume from last year that made him look like a clown. There were all sorts of funny acts he could do, like grown-up clowns perform during carnivals.

They planned to meet secretly in Jasmina's stall every day until all was ready.

There was a great deal to talk about, and much to do. For each of them got a new idea every few minutes. There was so much confusion that Tatu said they would have to make a program and then stick to it. So he brought pencil and paper, and wrote down exactly what they were going to have. José said that Tatu should be the manager, and Joa agreed. But now the fair was growing so much bigger than the way she had thought of it at first, and there were so many things to make, that they had better quit talking and get to work. As for her, she was beginning Guapo's suit right away.

"What are the children doing down there in the stable all the time? What's going on?" Mamai asked Papai.

Papai went out on the back porch to look, and came back with his finger on his lips. He was laughing.

"It's a big secret between them and Tarzan and the monkey," he said.

"What kind of a secret?" Mamai was full of curiosity.

"I don't want to know," said Papai. "And don't you go trying to find out, either, Mamai, or I'll never speak to you again." He pinched Mamai's cheek as if she were Joa.

Before he stopped listening, Papai had heard Joa scolding Guapo and telling him to stand still. She had cut out his little coat and basted it. He loved it so much that he kept pulling at the goods so she could scarcely try it on. And she was afraid she would stick him with a pin.

"I'm not going to make real trousers for him," she announced.

"He'll never let you fit them on him," said Tatu, looking up from lettering the fortune cards.

"No, he won't. I'll just make him romper pants. That'll be good enough for him."

"Let's see how he looks in his hat." Tatu put the hat on Guapo's head and the monkey pulled it off to see it. Then he tried to put it on again over one ear. Joa straightened it, and said surely he looked too cute for words. Guapo thought so too, and jumped around delighted with himself. Tatu said this was an act by itself. Now, if he would only do that the day of the fair!

Just then Maria looked in at them. She had come out into the quintal to pick some limes. She certainly was surprised to see Guapo in his costume. And she listened very seriously while the children explained all about the fair. She swore she would keep the secret. And she said she could help a lot, too. For instance, she could make paper rosettes and wreaths of flowers for decorating the animals and actors. She knew how to paint Jose's face like a clown, and she would try to think up some good things for her brother and sister to do—if Tatu and Joa wanted Sara and Tomás to take part.

Of course they wanted Sara and Tomás. That would be fine.

And thus their troupe of actors grew. It was going to be such a big show that they would have to invite a lot of people. And Joa said she would like to ask some of the girls she played with in town sometimes, the same ones who had sung the pastorales last Christmas.

So she made a special trip to visit Dona Josefina. And pretty soon quite a lot of people knew about the fair.

But just the same, when Tatu and José thumb-tacked notices on the veranda posts the day before, it was still a great surprise to Mamai, Papai, Sr. Diogo, Alzira and the neighbors who passed by, all of whom were invited to be present at four o'clock the following day.

Chairs and benches from the house and the garden were set in rows at the dining end of the veranda. Sr. Diogo and Papai attended to that, for some of the benches were heavy. There were not enough seats yet, so mats were spread on the floor in front for Joa's friends.

The other end of the veranda was the stage. And the hammock room was the entrance to that, with Maria in charge as wardrobe woman and stage hand.

The seats filled up rapidly. No one would have missed it for worlds. Only Sr. Diogo was missing when the hour struck. And he was out back of his house, starting the parade. Presently he blew a blast on his cow horn. This was the signal for Maria to start up the band record on the phonograph just inside the open door of the hammock room.

The band blared and the procession appeared. First came Tatu, mounted on Branquissimo. He was wearing his best white suit and a plug hat made out of cardboard. On one shoulder sat Pepe and Nene. And on the other was Guapo, dressed in his everyday suit of gray fur. Tatu carried a banner and two Brazilian flags waved from either side of Branquissimo's bridle.

Just behind marched Peixe-Boi, his horns wound in red crepe paper and trimmed with red rosettes; Maria's wreath of flowers was around his neck. To make sure the bull wouldn't start off on some notion of his own, Sr. Diogo had fastened a lead rope to his nose ring and handed Tatu the other end of it. This, too, gave the clown on his back a chance to perform. For riding Peixe-Boi was none other than José, although at first no one recognized him under his red and white make-up. José stood up on the bull's broad back which was like a table. He made some fancy steps, bowed to the crowd and then pretended to lose his balance. He was a pretty good clown and Peixe-Boi, who loved being the center of the show and was something of a clown himself, made a hit, too, in the parade.

Next came Sara in a pink crepe-paper ballet skirt, perched bareback on Jasmina. And after her was Maria's wonderful idea, which was the gayest and last thing in the parade. Maria had dressed up her father's white mule with garlands of flowers. She hitched him to a cart which she had decorated with a canopy of palm leaves and more flower trimmings.

Astride the mule was Tomás in his last year's red carnival

suit. He was steadying a pole on which Perla and Boy perched. When Perla heard the band, she began a shrill tune of her own, and Boy joined her in his loudest voice.

And in the cart was the lion tamer—Joa! She was posed with a big bull whip over Tarzan, who was securely tied to the top of a high stool. He sat comfortably on a green velvet pillow blinking at Joa and wondering what she was going to do. After his training the last few days, he was ready for anything.

The company on the veranda hadn't expected anything so fine as this parade, and they kept on applauding long after Joa and her cart had disappeared around the other corner of the house.

In a moment Tatu appeared on the stage, and announced the first number on the program. He began like a real circus manager, with "Respeitavel Publico!" which means "My Honored Public." He said that Sr. José de Tapajoz, the world famous gymnast, would now favor them with his daring act. Maria brought out a straw mat and kept the phonograph going softly. José turned a few summersaults, walked on his hands, stood on his head, and then balanced himself with Mamai's parasol across the rungs of a ladder laid on two chairs. Of course he clowned it, playing that he was about to fall every second or so. And Tatu chased him off the stage with a slapstick.

Tomás came on then, pulled a long rubber snake out of Tatu's pocket, and a toy white rabbit out of his plug hat, which embarrassed the manager so he sneaked away and hid. That gave Tomás a chance to recite a comic poem. He hurried to repeat the last lines when Tatu reappeared to stop him,

and let Sara come prancing around the stage on a broom-
stick hobby horse, picking up dropped handkerchiefs, like
a rough rider.

Joa and Tarzan were next, Tarzan on a leash, and Joa
carrying a fancy hoop. Even Tarzan didn't know what he
was supposed to do until Joa produced a mechanical mouse
from her pocket. It was wound up. And the instant she set
it on the floor on the other side of the hoop, it ran and Tarzan
leaped through the hoop after it. Then Joa pulled the mouse
by its string to the other side of the hoop. And the wild kitten
jumped after it again. Back and forth Joa kept Tarzan jumping through the hoop until he began to look bored. Then she
gathered him up and had him take a bow, while the audience
gave him a big hand.

Now came the most thrilling act of the show, according to
Tatu's announcement. It would be blood curdling, but the
Respected Public need not be alarmed for they would be in
no danger, while the actors were risking their lives.

Whereupon José and Tomás came out of the hammock
room door lugging a large chicken crate. They placed it on
the stage and ran away as if scared out of their wits. A pair of
wide jaws with terrible teeth thrust themselves into view.
Then followed the horrible head of an alligator slowly crawl-
ing out of the crate. No one could see the thin black fish-line
with which Maria was making Papai's stuffed alligator (the
one they had bought back in Itaituba) act alive.

Suddenly the entire troop of boys and girls rushed in,
brandishing wooden guns and daggers. The alligator lashed
his tail and leaped about. The hunters screamed and banged
away with their firearms. Tatu pulled off his coat, and used it

like a bull fighter's cape. He flashed it first on one side of the grinning jaws, then on the other, while Maria jerked the fish-line this way and that. It was surely terrifying.

But gradually things quieted down. The great alligator hunt was over. The 'gator lay still on his back, and the actors lined up to accept the applause. After they were gone, Maria dragged the stuffed beast off with her string, and the boys came and got the chicken crate.

So far no one had said anything about money, but troupers had to live. And it was time for Guapo to take up the collection.

Tatu had Maria's coffee grinder fixed up with a cloth over it, for the hand-organ. Guapo knew how fetching he looked in his red checked suit and straw hat, with the basket tied to his wrist so he couldn't drop it. While Tatu turned the crank and the phonograph played a jingling air, Guapo saw all the people looking at him and began jumping up and down with glee, just the way he had when he was dressed up in his costume the first time. He did quite a monkey dance. When Tatu led him up and down the rows of seats, he picked up every coin that dropped in his basket, turned it over and thinking it might be good to eat, started to put it in his mouth. It looked as if he were going to bite it, to make sure it wasn't counterfeit. And this sent the audience into bursts of laughter. Papai and Tatu's fishermen friends held their sides. And even Mamai had to get out her handkerchief to wipe her eyes. This made the collection go so slowly that Tatu finished it himself by passing his plug hat.

Tatu thanked the Respeitavel Publico for their generosity. He was glad they had enjoyed the program which was almost over. And he hoped they would take the opportunity to visit the managerie of wild animals from all over the world. Admission free.

And now, the renowned Ladies' Chorus of Santarem was about to favor them with a selection which would close the performance. Would the ladies please step forward?

The ladies did. They sang a brand-new song which Dona Josefina had taught them for the occasion. And that was the end.

While Maria started up the band record, Tatu hurried to the back porch to be ready with his fortune telling. Pepe refused to have anything to do with this. He only sat and stared at the people. But Nene was very obliging. She perched on Tatu's finger and every time he had a customer she picked out an envelope with a fortune card in it. Of course she knew there was a crumb of sugar stuck to each one, which she carefully took in her beak before she gave the envelope up.

At last the fair was over. Before they went home everybody had said it was a marvelous success, and that made the actors proud and happy. But Joa should have most of the credit, the children said, for it had been her idea.

"No," Joa insisted. "It was Papai's idea in the first place. He was teasing Tatu about needing only a hand-organ and a fortune-telling outfit to take to the fair and make a lot of money. Don't you remember that, Papai?"

Papai nodded. "Well, and did you make a lot of money?" he asked. "Where is it? I want my commission."

They had forgotten all about their collection. Tatu ran to fetch it; they spread it out on the back step, and counted it. There were twenty-one cruzeiros and some coppers. It looked like a lot.

"How are you going to divide it evenly among five of you?" Papai wrinkled his forehead at them, as they started putting it in equal stacks. He reached into his pocket and began counting his own coins.

"Here's my commission." Whereupon, Papai added some money to the piles and told them to begin counting over again. "Now you have twenty-five cruzeiros, which is five apiece. Pretty good business I should say. It will buy you all a lot of ices."

XVII

Digging in a Rainbow

ONE BRIGHT SUNNY morning, a few days after the excitement of the fair had died down, big drops of rain began to fall. They kept on coming down for about fifteen minutes while José and Tatu watched, blinking their eyes in the bright sunlight. Nothing of interest to equal the fun of getting ready for the fair had happened now for almost a week.

"Now would be a good time to hunt for Indian relics," said José.

"Why?" asked Tatu. "That little bit of rain didn't amount to much." He thought that a trip to the aldeia would be fun, however.

"Enough to pack down the dirt, but yet not too wet to dig."

"Well, let's go anyway," replied Tatu hopefully. He hadn't found a real Indian relic for his collection since the day he discovered the pumice-stone head, and he knew the time was getting shorter for the Amarals' stay in Santarem. "You get the trowels and a big sack," he said to José, "and I'll get Branquissimo. Let's start right away."

In a few moments Branquissimo, with José and Tatu

astride him, was running a race with the shower. It ran just ahead of them. Now they could see it coming down on the paved street of Santarem but not a drop was falling on them. By the time they reached town the rain had passed on, pouring great drops of water on the aldeia. Branquissimo did not seem to have much chance of winning this race though, for the shower hurried on into the woods much faster than even the horse's quick pacing legs could carry them. As though laughing and wishing to dazzle them, the shower left in its wake a beautiful double rainbow.

The boys could see the far ends of the two bows resting on the other side of the river. But the near ends hovered right over the thatched houses so that the roofs were splashed with rose and violet and green. José and Tatu were riding right into the gorgeous colors themselves.

"Oh!" gasped Tatu, delighted. "I've never been inside even one rainbow and I've never seen two of them."

"No?" José's dark eyes showed his amazement. "Why, they often come in pairs around Santarem. Haven't you ever really been inside a rainbow before?" He always seemed surprised when Tatu hadn't seen anything familiar to him because he felt that his friend had traveled so many miles that he must have seen about everything by this time.

"Oh, no, never! Let's get off right here," Tatu exclaimed excitedly. The air sparkled all about him, dazzling his eyes. He put out his hand as though to pick up a handful of the color. "Whoa, Branquissimo!" he said softly to the horse, afraid of breaking the spell.

José didn't seem half so excited. He started in to get the trowels. He was all for getting to work.

Tatu was still gazing, fascinated. "It wouldn't be fool's gold this time," José heard him saying.

"What are you talking about?" said José, with trowel in hand.

"I think there would be two, one for each of us, at the end of two rainbows. Come, let's look for the pots of gold, José. It must be true, it sparkles so."

"Oh!" laughed José. "So that's why you're in such a fog! Do you believe that old story about pots of gold at the end of the rainbow? Nope, you can't get me to waste any time looking for them. I've been fooled too much on tales like that. Nothing to 'em." And with that, José started in to use his trowel.

But Tatu felt that there must be some others who were searching for pots of gold, too. Other boys who were already there turning over the earth in the big empty lot looked to him like characters out of a fairy story. Their faces and clothes were gilded with the strange light inside the rainbows just as though they were enchanted creatures. He was afraid to mention this, however, for he didn't want José to laugh at him again. Leaving Branquissimo, who by this time was happily munching green grass but looking like a rainbow horse, Tatu followed along slowly until his friend picked out a choice spot for the digging.

Gradually the colors faded. The other boys and José became ordinary fellows again. Branquissimo was really only very white and the houses were only wet straw shacks. The arc in the sky seemed farther and farther away, and then it disappeared altogether. Tatu sighed a bit. He wanted double rainbows to last—for him and José.

But the time was short and there was much to do. Tatu began to work in earnest then. Could that little speck of pink peeping up through the top of the damp ground be a treasure, an Indian pot perhaps, better than a pot of gold? Long minutes passed and Tatu stuck to his task of digging. Most of the specks turned out to be ordinary pieces of stone or bits of broken dishes of which he and José had found a good many before.

Suddenly his trowel struck a point of hard gray rock that seemed to have a different shape than the others. After a few minutes of frantic digging, helped by José who came over in answer to his excited shouts, Tatu held in his hand a beautifully made ax—a real Indian tool, the first one he had ever owned. Now it was José's turn to be excited. He was just as pleased about Tatu's find as though it had been his own. The ax seemed to bring them good luck, too, for by the end of the morning their sack was bulging and heavy with a nice collection of Indian relics.

Of course, when they emptied the sack back home on the steps, all the little objects were sticky with mud. Neither of them knew what he really had until the dirt was scrubbed away. Tatu began to feel that perhaps the things he had thought worthwhile were just like the pots of gold at the end of the rainbows, that José might laugh at him again.

But José began to explain what the different things were. While he talked he generously offered to trade anything that he had, for, he reminded Tatu, he would always be there to get more . . .

At that, both boys looked at one another very seriously. Far down south was Tatu's home and when Papai's work for the government was finished, they would be going back. Tatu would be going away, far from Santarem and its Indian relics —and José. But now, though each one knew what the other was thinking, neither of them said anything. They just looked at the treasures, now that the trading was over, and tried not to feel too sad about the time that was coming for good friends to part.

Tatu's treasures, now washed and dried, really made quite a show laid out on the back steps. Although he prized the ax the most, José reminded him that the image of the little god was probably the rarest find. Unfortunately the god had lost its legs but that didn't make it any less interesting. And there were lots of heads of pottery animals. There was a tapir with a snout as long as an elephant's that had not broken off. A mutum turkey still had a ruffle of wattles on his head. Tatu remembered that these two were native to Santarem, and that made them all the more valuable to him. Besides these, there were little pieces of fish and snakes and turtles and alligators. But none of them all in one piece.

"They were once parts of beautiful dishes the Indians made," said José. "When the white men came and conquered them, they broke up everything and ran away. Wasn't that too bad?"

Tatu of course agreed with him, because anyone could see how clever the Indian potters had been, and how wonderfully they had known how to model. While they were talking, Sr. Diogo came over to look at the collection.

"Yes," said he as he handled the little clay image, "the rain often brings the Indians' gods to light. But they are warning us, I think. That shower was just to remind us of what is to come. Now is the time that farmers and cattle men will be worried, for who knows when the rivers will swell?"

Tatu was not half so much interested in Sr. Diogo's talk about the coming rainy season as he was in watching the little god. The sailor's fingers, gnarled and roughened, seemed clumsy, and Tatu was afraid he might drop it on the steps.

"Of course," the old sailor went on, "it doesn't matter in the town. Santarem is always safe and pleasant, far enough away from the river's force. But the country families will have to move to higher ground. Every rainy season the rivers will drive the families with their cattle from the lowest lands."

As he put the god back on the steps, Tatu breathed a sigh of relief, then he began to think about what Sr. Diogo had been saying. The cattle? Why, yes, already the corrals of the dairy were wet and sloppy. To higher pasture? Did that mean José would have to go along with his grandfather and Peixe-Boi and Bonequinho—and all of them? Early this very morning Tatu had watched Sr. Diogo move the hollow square of logs higher up on the beach. Now the cows were eating their sweet grass right by their front gate. The calves no longer had any space left to take their carefree run. The waters were gobbling up everything.

And now Sr. Diogo was saying that he had about decided that the time had come to move all the cattle to high and dry pastures. Tatu looked over at José. But José's dark eyes were intent upon his grandfather's words. He knew what they meant. Tatu did not know all that the coming of the waters would mean.

Next morning, when Antonio and Pedro came across the river with their load of grass, José told Tatu and Joa that the cows had had their last feed.

"It is hard to get any more canaraná now," explained Pedro. It was their name for the false sugar cane that the cattle liked so much.

"Yes," added Antonio, "this morning we had to paddle from place to place before we could find enough, and then we had to cut it while standing in the canoe, which is hard to do. Not long now, and it will all be under water. Then there will be nothing for the animals to eat."

When the two grass cutters heard that Sr. Diogo had decided to move the cattle, they offered to stay and help. The cows were finished eating, but they stood around in the water, switching at flies and looking very miserable. They seemed to be waiting for something, but they didn't know what.

"The rain brought more than rainbows to the river, didn't it?" said Tatu to José as they stood close together watching the sad-looking cattle.

"Yes," smiled José, "the rainbows brought no pots of canaraná for Peixe-Boi and his family—only trouble."

"Is the upland farm very far from here?" asked Tatu slowly.

"Oh, not so very far away. But then you will be going home soon yourself and—" José didn't seem to know how to finish what he wanted to say.

"But—" Tatu started to say something when a sharp *Toot-toot-toot* from up the river pierced the air. They all turned, and there was a cheery litle boat puffing down the river. From its thin smokestack, sparks were shooting. It was towing a strange-looking object that seemed to be a wide barge with a fence around it. As it came closer they could see that the barge was really a floating corral, with a gate that stood open.

Nearing the shore, the boat stopped and gave a sharp *Toot-toot-toot* again. Sr. Diogo was standing on the bank. Now he had gotten into his canoe and was signaling to José, who had left Tatu and Joa a few minutes after he heard the boat's whistle. Now he was running up to the corral and letting the calves out, two at a time. Tatu and Joa went up to the veranda where they had a better vantage point. It began to look as though moving these animals was going to be very interesting.

By the time they joined Papai and Mamai on the veranda—they had appeared to find out about the boat whistle, too—and could see what was going on, Antonio and Pedro had tied ropes around the necks of each pair of calves as José let them out of the corral. Very quickly and easily, then, they lifted the calves into the canoe, whereupon they jumped in themselves.

Of course the calves were frightened. They stood on trembling legs, wondering what was happening to them. Pedro held on to their ropes and Antonio talked to them softly, telling them not to be afraid, apparently.

"This is the first boat ride those rascals have ever taken," said Papai.

"Oh, the poor things," said Mamai. "I'll bet they're frightened to death." She was thinking of how scared she had been the first time that Sr. Diogo took her to town in his other canoe, the one that was lost.

At least the calves' trip was short, not nearly so long as going into Santarem. It was really only a few yards from the bank over to the barge. Sr. Diogo paddled the canoe along swiftly, and before they knew what was happening to them, the animals were lifted quickly up through the gate into the barge. There the folks on the veranda could see them, standing on their trembling legs and wondering what it was all about.

All went well each time José opened the corral to let another pair through—until it was Bonequinho's turn. He had been left to the very last, for he never could behave like the others. He was by himself, for safety's sake. Of course he had thrashed around as they lifted him up, but just when Antonio had succeeded in quieting Bonequinho, just as they were almost up to the barge, the calf began to strain at the rope. Pedro had his hands full trying to help Sr. Diogo steady the canoe, and before he could pull the rope tighter, over went Bonequinho into the water!

Then such a lot of snorting and kicking and churning of water! The rope, tight around his neck, was nearly choking him. Antonio leaned over to try to lift him back in, and the canoe nearly upset. On the shore, poor Boneca was bawling loudly. This Bonequinho had turned out to be the worst calf she had ever had. Now he was going to hang himself, or drown. It would take more than Antonio to do anything with him.

Sr. Diogo started paddling back to shore, dragging poor Bonequinho along, of course. In a minute or two, the water was so shallow that the calf could struggle back on his four legs and stand up. Antonio helped hoist him back into the canoe and Pedro loosened the rope so the calf could breathe

again. Then both men held him tight. There was no reason
to, now, for Bonequinho had had enough excitement for
once. The bottom of the canoe was full of water. Both Antonio
and Pedro were soaking wet.

Boneca had stopped bawling, but she was walking out in
the water trying to see her baby that had caused so much
disturbance. She knew all about moving, of course, for hadn't
she done it every one of the eight years of her life? Now as
the leader, the oldest and wisest of the herd, she started out
into the stream and the rest of the cows followed her. They
too were anxious to know what had become of their calves.
Boneca would show them what to do.

By the time she reached the barge the water was half way
up her sides. It was as though she remembered from the other
years, for, without hesitation, she gave a jump and her fore-
feet sprawled over the edge of the boat. Then she wriggled
and squirmed until she was balancing on her stomach.

"Good for Boneca!" shouted Tatu, and he voiced the senti-
ments of the others watching from the veranda. Maria and
Alzira had joined the family now, and they all gazed fascinated at the cows floundering around in the deep water, led
by Boneca. She had kicked with her hind legs until they had
caught hold on the edge. In a moment or two she had pushed
herself the rest of the way inside. Safely aboard the barge, she
fairly flew over to Bonequinho, but was apparently content
to find him still all in one piece and unhurt. There was nothing left to do but to lick him dry again.

And now Antonio and Pedro stood by while the other cows
succeeded, one at a time, in climbing aboard after Boneca.
"Ally—oop! Ally—oop!" they sang out, encouraging them

when they hesitated. And sometimes they caught hold of their horns and helped pull them up.

Finally nobody was left except Peixe-Boi, who did not like this business at all. He came along slowly, with everybody coaxing him. This was not the kind of attention he liked.

"Ally—oop! Ally—oop! Up—up, Peixe-Boi!"

And up came the big bull's short front legs. He stood with his hind legs in the river, his front hoofs clutching the barge. He looked very sad. Try as hard as he could, he wasn't able to move an inch farther.

"Ah," sighed Maria. "Too much canaraná this year, Peixe-Boi. Last year you made it. Now you are too fat. The sweet canaraná and all those oily cotton seeds did it, silly fellow that you are!"

And Peixe-Boi did indeed look very silly as Sr. Diogo boosted him from the canoe. But even that didn't help. With a disgusted and despairing grunt, the great bull slipped back into the water. There was a big splash.

"What will they do now, Maria? Poor Peixe-Boi can't be left behind all by himself," cried Joa who had always had a soft spot in her heart for him, even though he had scared her so that first day when she lay asleep on the sand.

"Don't worry, child," replied Papai, "that Captain is ready to take care of bulls no matter how fat they are. Look!"

The boat was slowly turning around, bustling into position. Peixe-Boi was frantically clutching at the churning water. Suddenly a big derrick could be seen swinging out from the boat and stopped right over the bull. Antonio had cleverly swung a rope and caught it around Peixe-Boi's horns. Now the winches on the boat began to rattle, and down came a big hook at the end of a great chain. Antonio slipped it into the rope. The machinery rattled again, and those on shore gasped as the huge Peixe-Boi was dangled in the air, his four hoofs kicking, his eyes rolling. Things looked pretty bad for the once gay bull hanging there, until the derrick shifted and let him down in the middle of the barge, whereupon he walked gingerly over into a corner by himself.

"Oh, he must be hurt, the poor thing," cried Joa.

"Maybe his horns hurt a little," replied Papai, "but I think his feelings are hurt more than anything. He's probably cross because all the cows and calves were watching him look so silly. It will be hard for him to lord it over them now for awhile."

They could see Antonio scratching Peixe-Boi's back and trying to comfort him. While Joa watched to see that care was being taken of her big friend, Tatu slipped off to follow José. Sr. Diogo's canoe, having delivered all the calves, was now being packed with cooking utensils, a big supply of food and hammocks for him and José. Last of all he tossed two duffel bags on top of the big pile. One of the bags missed the pile and rolled right off into the water. Sr. Diogo calmly fished it out and put it up on the pile again.

"Won't your clothes be all wet now?" asked Tatu, for he had seen José and Sr. Diogo stuffing their clothes in these big bags.

"Mercy, no, my boy," replied José's grandfather. "Those bags are covered with lots of good rubber. I should know. I did it myself."

"How?" queried Tatu. He knew he shouldn't ask now that Sr. Diogo was so busy but he was always such a nice one to answer questions.

"Why, I just gathered the sap—" he replied in a tone of voice that said how very simple it all was—"and poured it over these sailor bags of mine until the canvas was soaked. Then I hung them in the smoke to dry. This I did many times, and when they were done, I just sprinkled them with tapioca flour that is fine and soft. Now they are not sticky but they are waterproof, see? They have enough air inside them to keep them afloat even when they fall overboard."

Tatu thanked Sr. Diogo for explaining about the bags and thought how nice they would have been on the launch. He must tell Papai. Where was he? And where had José disappeared to when his grandfather had begun to tell about the bags?

Everybody seemed to be talking all at once back there on the veranda. Tatu wanted some time alone with José, for, even though the wet-season dairy farm was not so very far away, he felt that the time was not far off when they themselves would be leaving, and he wanted to tell José how much he liked being his friend and how nice it was to hunt for treasures together in the rainbows.

"He's always said that he wants me to see the world," Tatu heard José's voice speaking out clearly to Papai.

"What's this? What's this?" interrupted Sr. Diogo, coming up on the veranda now to say good-by to the Amarals.

"Oh, Grandfather—" began José, turning to him with dark pleading eyes.

"Eh? And now what?" the old man said, looking from

Sr. Amaral and back again to José.

"Well," replied Papai, glancing over at Tatu, "I have just taken the privilege of asking your grandson what he thinks of my idea for you and him to come to pay us a nice long visit at our plantation in the south, after my work for the government is finished and we are back there again. It won't be long now, and of course we, too, must be moving on to higher pastures with the coming of the rains. I would like to know what you think of the invitation now—and I'm sure the children would," he finished, smiling at a wide-eyed Joa and Tatu.

José's eyes were fastened on his grandfather's wrinkled face. He was looking at him in an unbelieving way, as though it were beyond him to hope that they might travel all those miles.

"Well," replied Sr. Diogo, smiling now, "I don't know but what an old sailor wouldn't be grateful for such a nice excuse to go a-traveling. I do indeed get restless staying in one place. As for José—" and his grandfather turned and put his arm on the boy's shoulder, "I've always said that I wanted my grandson to see the world. So don't be surprised next season, to get a letter saying that we're coming."

José grinned from ear to ear. His eyes were dancing with excitement. While everyone was shaking hands and saying good-by before Sr. Diogo's canoe put out across the stretch of water to the waiting steamer, José slipped close to Tatu and squeezed his arm.

"Tatu," he whispered excitedly, "there was a pot of gold in those two rainbows! The rains come and we move on, but before the rains come again . . . I'll be traveling the same miles you did all the way back to your home. Good-by now for a little while, Tatu."

Before the boy could reply, he was off. They all watched Sr. Diogo and José board the little steamer, dragging the canoe aboard after them. Then they stood waving, leaning over the side as the sparks flew out of the thin smokestack. The boat gave its farewell—

"Toot—toot—toot!" and the three notes were cheery ones.

THE END